The Journey Home

Portraits of Healing

Gabriel Bron

iUniverse books may be ordered through booksellers or by contacting:

iUniverse
1663 Liberty Drive
Bloomington, IN 47403
www.iuniverse.com
844-349-9409

ISBN: 978-1-6632-2295-4 (sc)
ISBN: 978-1-6632-2283-1 (e)

Library of Congress Control Number: 2021909823

Print information available on the last page.

iUniverse rev. date: 06/09/2021

Contents

Part One: Entering

Bridge Night

The Prayer Room

The Diagnosis

Altered States

The Purge

The Systems Guy

The Mirror

Admission Day

1. Bridge Night

My mother gave me the name Gabriel. She liked the image of an archangel for a son, and since I was born on September 29th, the holy day of the archangels, she figured it was an omen. She told me that my name meant "Messenger of God." She always thought, even before I was born, that I was destined to be the family story-teller, the assigned "village griot," the person whose duty it is to chronicle the generational narratives, to channel the ancestors' voices.

It took me a while to embrace this role. I learned early on that not everyone is keen to take in the stories you're trying to construct. You know the old saying, "Don't shoot the messenger"? Well, that is actually my greatest fear, that somebody someone *will* literally shoot me because they don't particularly care for the story I'm telling. I've carried this fantasy through to its final conclusion. I can envision the coroner's certificate — *Cause of death: telling stories.*

I guess it's a risk I have to take if I want to honor my birthright. It's my calling, my *ikigai*, as they say in Japanese.

The story I'm being called on to narrate here is not really all that complicated, though it does involve more than a few characters and events and spans two or three generations. But because it's essentially a journey, you can basically jump in at any time and still taste the *rasa*, the elemental 'juice' of the story. One thing I've learned from storytelling is that *all* journey stories are triangulated, interconnected through the linked events, intertwined through the related characters in the story. It doesn't matter where you start, you'll eventually wind up bringing everything and everyone relevant into the picture. Spinning the wheel here, I'll just start with that night in late summer three years ago.

It was a steamy August evening in my parents' suburban neighborhood near Sharon Woods, in Cincinnati. My mother and father were at their friend's house for their monthly bridge night. In their later years, my parents had established a number of inviolable routines, like this one with Sophia and Larry, friends of theirs from church.

On the surface, the story begins with "giving up," but not in the pejorative sense of shrinking from one's duty or throwing in the towel because you're overwhelmed by your opponent. This is the kind of giving up in which you surrender to larger forces of nature than you have previously contemplated. You take a step back, in awe of the organizing principles of the universe and let in a kind of regenerative power that redefines everything you have known.

I believe that at some point in everyone's life, they simply give up. Give up pretending. The rules of the game they've been playing for so long just don't make sense anymore. During that August evening, it happened for my mother. She is really the central figure in this story, the protagonist they say in literary circles — and she would love that title — as she tended to propel *every* story forward.

Up until the first hand was dealt, Mom had been processing the entire routine, the entire game all very pleasurably: *Swish-shh-shh. Such a pretty motion, the cards sliding toward me. Soo-fll, shoo-flll, soo-flll. Aqua blue, the color of the ocean, reflections glittering. Pick them up one by one, arrange them, arrange them. Wait, arrange them, how? They're smooth and clean. Like plastic.*

I hear the chatter around me. Chuku-shuku-chuku-shuku. Words about cards. About games. It sounds like music. La-la-la-la. Everyone singing together. I love this game.

Arranging the cards in her hands, she chortles her customary chirpy refrain, "who dealt this mess?" Everyone chuckles. She looks around and then swallows hard. Something does not feel right.

She scooches a bit in her chair, brushes her nose as if shooing away a fly, trying to refresh the scene.

These are my friends. That's Sophia and Larry, and there's Daniel. They're arranging cards, too. They're all smiling. Hearts and diamonds and clubs. I like these words. They're so comforting to me.

"Two diamonds," she hears my father say from the other side of the table. Half beat. "Pass," Larry replies.

So musical. The way everything is orchestrated, flowing so freely. Zzt-zzt-zzt. Wait a minute. This all means something. Doesn't it?

Sophia puts a hand on her arm to remind her, "Emma? Your bid."

And then Mom looks up, startled: *Your what?* She squints at Sophia, who is now arranging her own cards. *Who? Emma? Oh! That's me. Now what?*

And the silence stretches, one beat, two beats, three beats, too long. Smiling quizzically, Mom meets their eyes, looking for answers, somehow knowing they were speaking a language she doesn't fully understand. Knowing that they are referring to some distant set of rules that have no meaning.

"I don't know… how to do… this," she says at last, raising her voice as loud as she could muster, though it was barely audible to the others.

Now Dad squints at her. They have played this game, done this routine, followed this script so many times. He chimes in cheerfully, as he has done before when she gets distracted, trying to snap her out of her momentary trance, attempting to redirect her. "Emma, it's your bid."

She realizes he is talking to her. His voice and the feel of the plastic, the fleeting images of glittering blue flashing across the table. *It means something, doesn't it? This secret language we've been sharing all these years.*

"I don't know what I'm supposed to do." She says this quietly, but with certainty, directed toward him. There was a note of contrition in her soft reply, but it was mainly a factual report.

Dad sits up a little straighter in his chair, his expression confused, but not annoyed. "It's your bid, Em. Just make a bid," he coaxes her. He calls her Em or Emmy or Emilie when he wants to change the mood.

But no, the Rules of Play had disintegrated. Sort of like a chocolate jigsaw puzzle in the hot sun. All the pieces melting together. The meaning that connected this sequence of actions had dissolved. The cues for participating, all gone.

Not only Dad, but the other two in the room, Larry and Sophia, were all at a loss for what to do next. Emma had always been the glue of every gathering she was part of. As the fifth of nine children in the Hofmann household, she was always at the center of every decision, advising her siblings on their various dilemmas. When Emma sat you down to tell you "the real story," to tell you what you needed to do, you listened. She was the group voice, the interpreter, the planner, the decider. If Emma didn't know what to do, everyone was paralyzed.

"I don't know how to do that," she says again, a bit louder this time.

And then she starts tearing up. "I don't know how to play this game."

A voice inside is monitoring what she was saying, yet somehow it is a beat or two behind what she is actually saying. *Is that my voice? Can they hear me? Am I saying this out loud?*

Dad struggles to cover for her, mumbling something to the hosts about Mom having a lot of stress recently, not feeling herself. Larry and Sophia smile politely, forgivingly, waiting for Daniel to decide on a course of action.

Dad is also unsure how to proceed. Though he was the unwavering physical and financial leader of the family, he depended on Emma for direction, for certainty, in virtually every area of their life. But his main role was the designated 'fire fighter' in the family, extinguishing whatever blazes the children or anyone else in their lives would ignite. And he was quite accomplished in that role. Whatever fire he was directed to snuff out, you could be sure he would get the job done. This was a fire.

He made the best decision he could under the circumstances. "Maybe we ought to call it a night," he pronounced. He stretched and feigned a yawn, standing up, not waiting for a confirmation that this was, indeed, the only thing to do.

He walked gingerly around the table to Mom's chair, placed his hand on her elbow and helped her up, as if asking her to dance for the first time. *"Come on, Em, let's go."*

And he waited for her by the door, in his ever-patient manner practiced over the years, while she hugged Larry and Sophia, and apologized. "I'm sorry. I just don't know what's happening to me."

She followed him home, down the sidewalk, her arm draped over his, clasping hands, interlocking fingers. This all felt very comforting and familiar to her, reminding her of the moment when he first touched her hand, so many years earlier, on their third date it was, as they walked along The Mill Creek, behind her house. She had just introduced him to her father, the rather formidable Wilhelm Hofmann, who had somehow nodded his approval of him after a short chat. The sun had just begun to set, and the fireflies along the bank were emerging, flickering their silent messages. He reached over for her hand, and she responded eagerly, folding her hand into his, feeling the warmth and strength, and knowing, even then, that he would always lead her in the right direction.

Now, following their aborted Bridge Night, things were much the same. They walked, more slowly now, along the darkened edge of the woods, a chorus of frogs chirping desolately from the unseen lake, beyond the rows of darkened trees, the orchestras of crickets tweeting their endless symphony. Then, as if on a cue from an orchestral conductor, out came a smattering of fireflies, glimmering in a random harmony, summoning them with their inviting amber light. The two of them made their way slowly up the narrow path to their home, Mom holding a bit more tightly onto Dad's arm.

2. *The Prayer Room*

I described my mother as the protagonist of the story, in the sense of being the person around whom everything somehow revolves. But my father is also a protagonist in the sense that he is the one who has the emotional breakthroughs and makes decisions that propel the story forward.

I would say that the first breakthrough was in the days that followed Bridge Night. My father would learn how to cry again.

I had only seen him cry once in my entire life, when I was about seven years old. Dad was doing some construction work on our garage behind our house, on a Saturday morning. He always had some bold new project to tackle on the weekends and would usually invite me or one of my brothers to participate. That day, he was building some kind of scaffold thing with steel pipes so he could reroof the garage.

I remember that he was jostling around a pile of iron rods, to remove them from a shelf, about at his eye level. I was standing by, kind of cheering him on, though there was nothing I could really do to help. As he tried to pull one pole from the pile, he took a deep breath and gave a massive grunt as he vigorously tried to pull it free. The pole suddenly catapulted out, the end bashing him on the forehead, right above his eye socket.

Dad let out an angry growl at the universe, an alarming sound of distress that I had never heard from him before. It might have been the first time I had ever seen him fail at something he was trying to do. After a moment, weird purplish goo started oozing out of his forehead. *Is that blood?* I wondered. My blood was bright red, but this was much darker and thicker.

I was amazed that my father could actually bleed. The sound he was making was a kind of crying, I guessed, but it felt wilder, more like the howling of the wolves we occasionally heard from the woods.

Dad fell to his haunches and continued moaning. I had no idea what to do. Through his clenched eyes, blood now soaking his forehead in little pulses, he made a wild circular motion with the index finger of his right hand, miming for me to call Mom to come help.

At that instant — *snap!* — I understood that crying was not a good thing. It indicated that you were weak. It showed that you had failed. It announced that you needed help.

"Mom, come here. Quick. Dad's bleeding!" I shouted, running toward the house. I then felt that by pronouncing this, I too was somehow complicit in the crime.

Bridge Night was another vicious steel pole whacking Dad in the forehead. In the days following that pivotal event, both Mom and Dad became much quieter than usual. Dad would start to say something, like a comment about the news or a note from one of the kids, but then he'd pause and think, *No, no need to bother her with that.* Mom would think about something she wanted to say, maybe an intention to visit one of her sisters or a dinner plan, but then she'd close her eyes, not finding the energy to articulate the thought, *No, no need to try to say that.*

A kind of mutual questioning hung over their relationship. Not a mistrust by any means, but a sense of being tested. And simultaneously, the mood was infused with a sense of calm acceptance: *Okay, now we've been through this. The worst is over. What else could possibly happen? Ha! We can laugh at this, right? Ha-ha, see, we survived this. Whew, what a scare, eh? Ha-ha-ha.*

Mom gradually resumed her usual routine, slowly taking up her regular social activities — church, shopping, and visiting her sisters and friends. Though now she did her activities always with Dad as chauffeur and chaperone and occasional interpreter. Dad, of course, had secretly hoped that Bridge Night was an isolated incident, an oddity, a one-off occurrence. But deep down, he knew it wasn't. Deep down, he knew he'd have to learn to cry again.

I didn't know it at the time of the pole thrusting incident, but I later learned the broad outlines of Dad's war experiences in the South Pacific, being captured and 'serving time' as a POW in the Philippines. He would never say much about it. "What else can I say?" he'd challenge me every time I'd ask for details. "It happened. It's over. There's no need to revisit it. Time to move on."

Some weeks after Bridge Night, the inevitable confirmation came. It was a Wednesday, around six o'clock. Mom was in the kitchen, preparing a simple dinner. She had a Tupperware container of leftover spaghetti sauce, taken from the refrigerator and now sitting on the counter next to the stove. She had opened a package of spaghetti and had stooped down to take a 2-quart sauce pan out of the cabinet for boiling the pasta. Standing up, she scanned the counter with the Tupperware container and the opened package. She looked down at her hand that was holding the pan, a pan that she had been using for over twenty years.

Dad hears Mom call from the kitchen. "Da-a-an, can you come here?" Mom's voice is shaking. Dad has often heard this kind of desperation in her voice. Mom would get flustered if she couldn't open a jar, or if she didn't have all of the ingredients she needed for a recipe. But this sounds a little different, a little more distressed, a little more desperate.

Dad waits a moment, sighs, lowers the volume on the TV news, releases his reclining chair to the floor. His feet hit the floor with a loud plop. He looks around the room, takes a final clanking gulp from his scotch on the rocks, then ambles toward the kitchen.

He pauses at the doorway to assess. "What *is* this?" Mom asks. She holds out the pan, her arm quivering. "I can't quite figure out what this is for."

Dad looks at her, alarmed. *Is she joking? Is that really what she just said? What* is *this?*

He gently takes the pan from her hand and places it on the counter.

"That's okay," he says calmly, placing his arm around her shoulders. "You're just tired, Emma. You go rest and I'll finish making dinner."

Mom walks slowly to her room, not her bedroom, but to her 'quiet room,' an extra bedroom in the house, next to the kitchen, the guest room that she had converted to a kind of prayer room. The walls were lined with framed inspirational drawings and quotes ("Lord, make me an instrument of your peace…"), the tables piled neatly with prayer books and religious magazines (*The Catholic Telegraph, Mission,* and several others). Though Dad has scarcely registered it, Mom has been spending more time alone in her prayer room recently. Since that night at Larry and Sophia's, she had spent hours on end there, not joining Dad to watch his nightly TV shows: *Jeopardy, Wheel of Fortune*, or the *WLWT News*. While he thought it was a bit odd, he knew that she had her own separate interests — they didn't need to do everything together.

When Dad finishes preparing dinner that day — heating up the water for the spaghetti and heating the pasta sauce — he walks to the door of the prayer room to let Mom know it is time to eat.

He had been hoping for the usual scene: Mom seated on the small couch or in her rocking chair, head bowed, reading quietly from a prayer book. But this time, she isn't sitting in her rocking chair or on the couch. She is standing at the window, her hands joined in prayer, faint beams of the sunset light on her shoulders, reciting flawlessly one of the many prayers she knew. That she knew by heart. Her native language.

The whispery tones of her prayer voice emanate from the room. *Shu-shu-shu...* "Though I am but a prodigal child, I appeal to you and shu-shu... Please listen to my prayers and shu-shu-shu... See my contrite heart, and shu-shu-shu... Please help me now and at the hour of my death. Amen."

She repeats the prayer. Again. And again. Her body swaying rhythmically, as if doing a solo dance, an elegiac performance. Dad has seen her like this before. She is a natural dancer and she can make any routine action look as if it has been elegantly choreographed. But this time there is a note of desperation.

Dad wets his lips, inhales, searches for his own voice. "Emilie, are you okay?" He uses "Emilie" rather than Emma whenever he wants to wake her from some reverie. The question echoes across the expanse of the hollow room. Eventually, she turns slowly and smiles at him, astonished that he had suddenly appeared in the room.

Dad smiles in response, then closes his eyes, recalling the woman he has seen so many times in this room, reverently bowed in quiet reflection. When he opens his eyes, he is astonished also. Astonished at the quiet, at the late afternoon shadows. Astonished how separated she has become, how inward she is. Realizing that some things would need to be revisited. Alarmed that he would need to learn to cry again.

3. The Diagnosis

Pine, catalpa, pin-oak, persimmon
But not tree
Hummingbird, hoot-owl, martin, crow
But not bird
Cannas, honeysuckle, cockscomb, rose
But not flower

Growing up in a Catholic German-American household, I learned the power of language rituals, linguistic precision and the potency of labels. "It's not *a flower*, honey," my mother used to say, ridiculing the simplicity of such a basic word. "It's so much *more* than that. It's a dianthus, or you can call it a Sweet William or a Rockin' Red… but *not* just a flower."

What you call things had come to take on a great deal of importance, and a lot of our family rituals were based on naming and renaming things, and then seeing how others reacted to our lexical choices. We've always prided ourselves on word play, banter, badinage, persiflage, repartee.

One word game that my brothers and I would play as kids was the 'Would you rather' game. "What would you rather have — a charley-horse in one leg that would last the rest of your life or a red-hot poker stuck up your nose for ten seconds?"

"Would you rather use eye drops made of vinegar or toilet tissue made from sandpaper?"

We prided ourselves on coming up with the most vulgar comparisons.

Mom would often overhear us playing this game, let out a mock clucking sound, roll her eyes, and sigh, "Oh, you boys!"

We'd laugh and laugh at the silliness of the game, and then roll in laughter some more that we were able to get to her. *Made you laugh, made you laugh!*

I think all diagnoses of illness are a version of this 'Would you rather...?' word game. You can always find a silver lining in what the diagnosis is *not*.

"Thank God, at least it's not a *spirometra mansoni* flatworm living inside your liver!" You can be thankful for that!

Mom's diagnosis was reported in a very clinical, dispassionate manner, almost cruel in its intended finality. *Wait, say that again... You mean, all of this is just... that word?*

That's right. That's what it is. I've named it now. My job is done.

The diagnosis had been sitting there for some time, waiting to be proclaimed. After Dad had discovered Mom in her Prayer Room that evening, quietly reciting her invocations, he decided to call my older sister Kate.

Now if you're trying to follow the story in terms of literary archetypes, you'll soon recognize that Kate is the 'hero' — or more accurately the 'heroine.' You will soon see her with all of her strength, courage, honor, and whatever other noble qualities heroes are supposed to possess.

But in terms of practicality for this episode, you just need to see Kate for her visionary attributes. Kate had always been the family diagnostician, able to expose the true source of many a personal problem.

Kate lived nearby and Dad knew she would come immediately, so he pondered: when, when, when to call her. Not now, no not now, not yet. He decided on later that evening, yes, later, after dinner, maybe around eight. Not right away, of course, don't want to sound too desperate. Dad realized he was repeatedly whispering to himself, "What to do, what to do?", his own version of prayer.

Now, around seven Mom had gone to lie down, having eaten only a few bites of her dinner, complaining of not feeling well.

He bumped the planned call to 7:15. It was a call Dad had never wanted to make, had never dreamed of making.

He was in desperado mode, channeling a bit of what he recollected of S.O.S. calls from his days in World War II. *du-du-Du, duu-duu- Duu, du-du-Du.* Short-short-short, long-long-long, short-short-short — Morse Code encryption. It's an ambigram — you can understand it backward and forward, right side up, upside down. Emergency Distress Signal. *Don't make this call unless you know you're going down. Save our souls.*

"It's your mother," he said when Kate picked up the phone. "Can you come over? She's…"

He was uncharacteristically tongue-tied. Not like him. Aposiopesis. Inability to finish the thought. Pregnant silence.

He was trying hard to navigate around saying the obvious, "something is wrong."

This was the moment of truth. For months, Dad denied Mom was having any problems out of the ordinary, and now was conceding that she should be 'assessed.' *Wait a minute, did I just say that: Assessed?* A really awful word, an appalling concept for Dad to digest. All his life, Dad had preached distrust of authorities, of government regulations, of anyone by whatever title claiming to know something he didn't. It was one of his 'rules,' something he learned from his father, my grandfather Jake, who could *hurumph* the authorities with the best of them. You have to find your own solutions, not to depend on 'the specialists.'

But the Bridge Night Incident ("I don't know how to play this game anymore") and the Kitchen Incident ("I don't know what this is for") convinced him. Mom's condition was now leading him into new territory. It was indeed hostile terrain. His military thinking about self-preservation — a collection of often contradictory rules — kicked in:

Rule #1: Don't die on the battlefield.

Rule #2: Don't leave a dying comrade on the battlefield.

Rule #3: Don't ever entertain the idea of death.

As a World War II veteran, a proud soldier of the 37th Infantry Division (a.k.a. The Buckeyes), Dad knew that the call for reinforcements was not something that you took lightly.

Rule #4: Call for reinforcements only when death is imminent.

Rule #5: When death is inevitable, face it proudly.

None of his training through 'the rules' he learned from his father or the military codes he learned in the army would help him with a practical problem like this. The training would only help him brace for what was next.

But Kate was on it. She made an appointment to see Dr. Patel, Mom's regular doctor, the very next morning. "Sure, bring her in. We can fit her around noon," Dr. Patel's nurse said, as cheerfully as if Mom were coming in with a thorn under her thumbnail.

For Kate, having to schedule this visit was not particularly upsetting. She had been seeing the signs in Mom for months. She had been witnessing what she called "the progression." The rest of us had seen signs of absent-mindedness and forgetfulness, but we'd remind ourselves: she's *always* been that way. Even when we were little, it was not uncommon for her to say things like, "hey, you — Liam, Gabe, Theo, whatever your name is — take this laundry basket down to the basement."

The visit went as expected, per protocol. Dr. Patel asked Dad and Kate questions about Mom's memory:

- Does memory loss disrupt her daily life — such as interfere with doing things with other people?
- Does she have challenges in planning things or in solving problems, like opening a package or doing simple arithmetic?
- Does she have problems with familiar tasks like brushing her teeth or preparing meals?
- Does she have a harder time following stories?

Does she...? Does she...? Does she...?

Dad's spirits drooped with each question. *Yes...Um, yes, I guess so... Um-hmm, yeah, yes, that too.* The answers were *all* "yes." For each query, he had some sort of counter though: "No, not so often." "Oh, maybe occasionally." "Mmm. That might happen but only when she's really tired." "Well, yes, but it's not a big deal." "I guess so, but she's always been kind of like that."

Eventually though, Dad had to concede that *all* of the signs were present. Not only present, but explicit, trenchant, indisputable, irrefutable.

Dr. Patel said he'd like to take Mom into the examination room and that he'd be back in a few minutes. Dad waited silently, next to Kate, half-staring down at the sliver of light seeping under the bottom of the examination room door. Usually, in a situation like this, he would fidget, wander around the room picking things up to examine them, maybe pull out a crossword puzzle book. But not this time.

In the quiet of the examination room, Dr. Patel asked Mom the usual diagnostic questions. "Emma, where are we now?" "What month is it?" "What season is it?" In language teaching, these are called 'display questions.' You know the answers, but you're just checking if your subject is processing the language correctly.

Mom did not feel like she was a student in a foreign language class. Instead, she felt like she was on trial. She knew it. *Your words are passing me by, but I know what you're trying to do. You can't fool me.*

Dr. Patel would have shown her some objects — a pen, a phone, a cup, maybe — and asked her to name them in sequence. He would have asked her to count in reverse or maybe spell some words backwards. He would have asked her to repeat some unusual idiomatic phrases: "more bang for your buck," "double whammy," or maybe, "the best thing since sliced bread." He would have given her some simple instructions to follow. A series of little pop quizzes, probing different areas of her brain. For each little task, Mom might stumble, or squint or shrug. The prize pupil, 'Straight-A Emma,' who always prided herself as an impeccable student, was flunking the test. She knew it.

It didn't take long for Dr. Patel to lead Mom back into the office where Dad and Kate waited in silence on the other side of his desk. Dad looked the doctor square in the eye before he spoke, trying to reach a gentlemen's agreement: *Please let it be something else.*

Dr. Patel entered easefully, sat gingerly behind his desk, and smiled wanly at Dad and Kate. Using his gentle bedside dialect, he spoke softly, "Well, we'll do some tests to rule out blood clots or a tumor." Everyone is comforted by a Plan B, however outlandish it might be.

In Dad's mind, an exotic diagnosis would have been the *best* possible news under the circumstances. *Yes, please let it be something you can view under a microscope.* Something that we can identify, correct, excise, eliminate. Some enemy that we can attack, crush, eviscerate.

Maybe *Chaaetorimum Strumarium*, a rare black mold that causes memory loss? We could isolate its location, maybe in the air conditioning system in our house and treat it. Or simply burn down the house.

But then Dr. Patel continued, "In my professional judgment, Emma has a significant loss of cognitive function. This is Stage 1 Alzheimer's."

This was not what he wanted to hear. He didn't want to hear this word. Ever. Not in this lifetime.

The walk back to the car was quiet, deliberate, as if trekking through molasses. Dad helped Mom into her seat, and even pulled her seatbelt over and clicked it in place. Then he gave her hand a squeeze. "You'll be all right, Em. You'll be all right."

"He's *such* a nice man," Mom said as they pulled out of the lot.

Dad drove along Lebanon Road, along Sharon Woods, awash with the glory of red-tipped leaves dangling from the limbs of Buckeye trees, reminding that summer was now past, that fall was upon us, winter inevitably arriving, and the cycle would inevitably repeat intact, safe, untouched by human drama.

Did she mean me, or Dr. Patel who's nice? Dad wondered. He glanced over at Mom, who was clutching at her seatbelt strap, staring at the abundance of trees in the woods, mesmerized as if seeing this brilliant color for the first time.

Dad smiled. *It doesn't matter,* he thought, exhaling deeply with relief for the first time in weeks. *She's thankful, she's grateful, she's alive.*

I don't know what to call this, he thought to himself, *this new relationship. But at least we have one. We don't need to name it right now. We don't need to know its name.*

4. *Altered States*

By now you know the protagonists in this story — that would be Mom and Dad — and the heroine — that's Kate. You also know the narrator-slash-messenger — that's me, Gabriel. So you may be wondering, "Well, then who's the *antagonist*?" In pure literary terms, the antagonist is the person who actively opposes or is hostile to the protagonist. In short, an adversary, someone who persistently 'stands in the way.'

You might propose that Dr. Patel is the antagonist, but that would be the same kind of shoot-the-messenger error as if you think the narrator is the bad guy. Or you might assume that the antagonist isn't a guy at all.

It must be Alzheimer's! Yes, dementia is the antagonist and that the characters will rally against it and defeat it. *Rah-rah-rah.*

But alas, that is wishful thinking! We are a species of dreamers. *Pium desiderium.*

The dementia is certainly an *obstacle*, but it's not the adversary, not the antagonist. The antagonist in this story is our resistance: our resistance to understand the course of nature and our resistance to embrace aging and decline as an actual ally on our journey.

In biochemistry there is *another* definition of antagonist: a *substance* that interferes with or inhibits the physiological action of another action. And as a species, *homines sapientes* — humans who are wise — we are continually evolving new ways of inventing antagonists. That's how smart we are! We can always formulate ways of inhibiting and altering natural processes. It's what we do.

Be careful what you wish for.

I think we are all tempted to seek altered states of consciousness. Care for a bite of this apple? A promise of something more? Something better?

By the time Mom's Alzheimer's diagnosis emerged, I had been fully aware of how to induce altered states. I had come to respect the transformative power of 'antagonist drugs.' The power to change things, to metamorphose my experience of the world.

So given that Mom's 'experience of the world' was deemed 'deficient,' Dr. Patel prescribed a barrage of medications to "help her through this." Caution: *Homo sapiens* at work.

The notion of 'help' is a bit tricky. *Help who? Help her? Help Dad? Help Dr. Patel?* It didn't seem to matter. The idea of external assistance sounded promising. We were all — my father, my four siblings, and I — complicit in the decision, though no one recalls giving an enthusiastic endorsement, "Yes, let's do this!"

And we all found our individual ways to dance around and with the antagonist. For me, it took quite a while for Mom's Alzheimer's diagnosis to sink in, to become part of my reality. I rehearsed different ways of talking about it with others in my world: *Mom? Oh, she's doing really well. Better than ever!* (misdirect) *My mother? Oh, she's okay.* (complete denial) *How's my mom doing? Not so well.* (partial denial) *How is my mother these days? Well, she's having some memory issues.* (euphemistic hedge) *How's Mom? Stage 1 Alzheimer's* (direct answer, with technical softening) *How's my mother? Hey, that's my mother you're talking about! None of your business!* (rebuttal).

Nothing sounded right. Logically, you know your parents are likely to leave this mortal coil before you do, and will likely undergo *some* decay before they depart, but you still hold on to the thought: *You're not going to die. I can't imagine life without you. You're never going to die.*

And we were all secretly hoping that some form of drug therapy would be our salvation, a 'magic bullet' as it were, to quiet the adversary.

And we all felt we needed to do *something*. We certainly didn't want to be negligent. Another face of paranoia creeps in: *We, the jury, sentence the entire family to life in prison for neglect.* So we were willing to experiment — with Mom's psyche: What the magical pharmacopeia world was offering her was a *possible* relief from the symptoms, a temporary diversion, an altered state.

We repeated the mantra to each other: No cure exists, but medications may temporarily *help*.

Sometimes the little yellow Aricept pill helped Mom feel light and communicative. Like her old self, more on top of things. But sometimes it made her dizzy, sometimes fatigued, sometimes nauseous. Often, it made her extremely constipated.

Sometimes the spongy orange Exelon capsules helped her remember things, follow conversations and stories and TV sitcoms with greater attention. But often it gave her insomnia and prompted her to walk around during the night, hallucinating.

Sometimes the powdery, cranberry red Galantamine tablets helped Mom sleep through the night and have less terrifying dreams. But it sometimes gave her shortness of breath and an irregular heartbeat.

Sometimes the chalky blue, football-shaped Zyprexa tabs helped decrease her hallucinations and fits of paranoia. But they also led to a shriveling weight loss.

The question for Dad, for Kate, as they observed her under the influence of her medications was: *Where did she go? Where did she wander off to today?*

Mom herself was skeptical of the medications. She would say things like, "this pill is too small. How can this do any good?" Or "This pill has such a strange color. How will it possibly help me?"

And that eerie question kept popping up when things didn't go well: *Who the hell gave you the right to do this to me?* Flashback: When I was in the Peace Corps in Togo in West Africa, I had scrupulously avoided any illegal drugs, though they were readily available. I had heard that any run-in with the Togolese military/legal system could be a life-wagering coin toss. But I did become rather fond of *sodabé*, the West African palm wine that you drank from small coconut shell shot glasses. *Sodabé* was widely consumed, cheap, and perfectly legal. The perfect elixir for preparing to meet any antagonist in your life.

Living near the ocean in Lomé, I would sometimes walk the beach late at night and visit one of the outdoor bars along the beach side of Rue Gnagbadé. One used to frequent, Café L'Oasis ('The Oasis'), offered a "*Sodabé Supérieur*" that seemed to have a little extra kick to it.

Some nights, after a visit to Oasis and a chat with the proprietor, Leopold, I'd wander along the ocean beach. One night I ambled all the way to Aného, until the light peeked up over the eastern horizon, illuminating the world in a sudden glimmer of blue. The shock of beauty. I felt that I had arrived in a magical place. I felt that my being here was *destined*, that there was no place else I'd rather be. I knew the *sodabé* had *something* to do with this realization, this liberation, this transformation.

It wasn't until much later, right before I was due to return to the States and I was making my good-bye rounds, that I discovered that the "Le Supérieur" was laced with *iboga*, a kind of psychedelic.

Monsieur Gabriel, je suis désolé si je t'ai accroché au iboga, Leopold said when I dropped in one evening to say farewell. "Mister Gabriel, sorry, if I got you hooked on iboga." Iboga?!

I was angry. *Who the hell gave you permission to do that to me?* I was dead serious, but Leopold just chuckled knowingly. *No way you couldn't have been aware of this!* Yes, he's right. I must have known. I gave him permission. Leopold was not the villain here. He was just the messenger.

Now on the eve of my departure, all is forgiven, our roles in each other's lives are sorted out. We share a farewell handshake, a ritualistic grasp ending with a finger snap by both of us. *Good luck, I'll miss you.* He smiles and responds in Éwé, the local dialect, testing my comprehension: *Gbe deka mede blibo o.*

Another lesson from Leopold: *One language is never enough.* We can learn something from every person whose path we cross, so it is best to understand their *native* tongue.

So now with Leopold just a vague memory — I can barely recall his face, though I do remember the touch of his handshake — I think of Mom, and her forced prescriptions of the little chalky yellow pills and the spongy blue pills and the powdery red pills.

Of course she's upset. She should be. *Who the hell gave you permission to drug me like this?*

I wish I could tell her: The drugs are not your adversary. The dementia is not your adversary. We will all face this experience together.

5. *The Purge*

Clink-a-thunk. Dad gingerly pitches the half-empty bottle of Macallan forty-year-old whiskey I had brought him from Scotland into the trash. A slight moment of regret, reconsideration, and then: *No, this is the decisive action.*

Next the *clatta-clatta* of a partially-filled bottle of Cutty Sark. *Ah, this is getting easier.* Then a nearly empty bottle of Ballantines, and then the Dewars — no regrets about how much is left in it. It's all got to go. Everything that had accumulated in his cabinets over the years. All crashing into a single amorphous heap in the green recycling bin he hauled in from the garage and placed in the middle of the kitchen floor.

As Dad tells it, the days following the diagnosis were very sobering for him. Literally. One Sunday afternoon, he pitched out everything in his various booze cabinets. "It's easier when *everything* is gone," he said.

This meant, of course, a number of lifestyle changes that had become embedded in his routine. No more ritual of the pre-dinner scotch-and-water on the rocks, no more opportunities for the one or two he might have swished around while watching TV in the evening. And when a friend or neighbor or relative stopped by, there'd be no "Can I get you a drink?" conversation opener.

I admired that he could just switch off lifelong habits like this, cold turkey. Years earlier, he had done the same thing with smoking, after going through a couple of packs of cigarettes a day since his army days, when it was practically mandatory for a man to smoke. As a kid, I always saw him with a cigarette. I assumed then that all 'real men' smoked, that it was a sign of adulthood, independence, self-sufficiency, immunity from pain, omnipotence.

Smoking had always been an extension of Dad's identity. I recall an endless procession of brands over the years, half-filled packs lying everywhere around the house and in Dad's workshop: the scarlet Pall Mall's that I remember Grandpa Wilhelm bumming from him, the cool red-and-black bulls-eye of Lucky Strike's with the cryptic "It's Toasted" motto, the really boring-looking Kent's, the long parallel ruby bars of Tareyton's, the brilliant crimson of the Winston pack with the gold eagle floating overhead, the emerald green Kool's with the interlocking O's, the turquoise-striped Newport's with their inverted swirl mark. I searched for a secret code in the brands of cigarettes that he smoked, hoping to find the hidden clue that made smoking these things so attractive.

I secretly wanted to be like my father. I tried imitating virtually every 'Dad meme' I could decipher, and smoking was, of course, one of the easier symbolic acts to figure out. I somehow felt if I could put together all of his 'Dad things', I would be baptized into some mystical state of manhood. I started filching his cigarettes when I was about ten years old, about the time I entered VYO baseball, C league. His cigarettes were strewn everywhere, and it was just too tempting not to try out this privileged pleasure — and I always figured there was no way he was keeping track.

Learning to hold a cigarette between my first two fingers, take a shallow inhale, suppress a cough, and *fwwww,* out through my lips. Very cool sacramental rite. A few like-minded buddies and I would alternate the thieving responsibilities from our equally-addicted fathers. Most often, we would smoke in the woods in a little ravine off of Murdock Road, behind Andrews Field. We'd take tiny puffs without inhaling, holding the burning cigarettes reverently. We'd nod our approval at each other's partaking, savoring our little secret society ritual.

The impetus for Dad to quit smoking was a visit to the doctor many years later, probably when he and Mom were in their sixties. The initiative was not by Dad himself — he didn't believe in doctors or the power of medicine — but by Mom. She had been having heart palpitations, first rarely, then more frequently. Dad was with her during her eventual diagnostic 'stress test' on the treadmill, in which the technician keeps viciously amping up the speed transducer of the walking belt in careful increments to see how your heart valves respond. At some point, everyone will either collapse or get launched off the belt, unable to keep up. But, like the eight seconds of riding a bronco at a rodeo, there's a passing criterion, like 160 heartbeats per minute, and if you reach that, the technician will slow down the belt to a stop and tell you that you passed the test.

After a few minutes of gradually accelerating speed, Mom was panting and slipping, heaving death rattles from her chest. The technician was dutifully making notes on his pad. Dad jumped up out of his chair to cut the test short.

"Got enough information?" he bellowed, as he punched the red emergency stop button himself.

She didn't pass the stress test.

Following Mom's diagnosis of 'premature ventricular contractions,' Dad decided, duly influenced by the brochure Mom's doctor handed him, that second-hand smoke may have been partially responsible for her condition. *Second-hand smoke? What the hell is that?*

Once he figured out that *he* was the source of this toxin, the decision was easy. No one had to tell him that it needed to be done. One day, he saw a sign. Literally, a sign. There's a concept in linguistics called 'Relevance Theory' which holds that our cognitive processes are ruled by one simple drive: we search for that which is relevant to us. So he noticed a sign on a company bulletin board. 'Quit smoking in one session.'

That's all it took. It was a single two-hour hypnotherapy session in a high school auditorium. I didn't find out the nature of his therapeutic treatment until much later. I had to pry it out of him. *How the hell did you quit smoking after forty years?* Dad would never admit that he 'succumbed' to some kind of New Age 'mumbo jumbo' like hypnotherapy.

But that's all it took. The next day, all the smoking paraphernalia went into the trash, including a rare hand-carved teak ashtray with a mythical dragon holding up the receptacle, something I had acquired in West Africa as a gift for him.

It's hard to shop for this guy. He always throws out these treasures I give him.

So cold turkey *does* work.

Following the session with Dr. Patel in which Mom received her Alzheimer's diagnosis, Dad was now purifying himself again, as a warrior might do in preparation for a major battle.

My older sister Kate, whose role as our parents' monitor, confidante, and caretaker, had ramped up in the past several months, was preparing herself for 'the steep decline.' She had started participating in support groups for people in similar situations: 'Caring for an Aging Partner or Parent,' 'Caregiving Support Network,' 'Friends Coping with Aging Parents,' 'The Honeymoon is Over.' Meetings in dank church halls mostly, drinking stale coffee with powdered creamer, just like in AA meetings. Kate had invited Dad to attend on multiple occasions, but he always balked, saying, "I've never really believed in that sort of thing."

Following the diagnosis, Dad had started calling me, his number three child, on the phone frequently "to catch up." I was taken aback. Why call me? Why not talk to Kate? Maybe it was because I was 'a guy' and

I understood his 'guy speak.' And probably more so than my two brothers, I had shown some interest in learning Dad's 'code,' "Jake's Rules" I came to call it, since it originated, or at least was certainly distilled to its current 100 proof rating by his father Jacob.

For instance, when we were alone and certainly out of earshot of Mom, Dad and I would often use the same vernacular to curse about things ("That's horseshit" was one of our go-to expressions.)

I'm pretty sure that Dad had tested my two brothers, Liam and Theo, on their ability to engage in 'Guy Speak' and cerebrate around 'The Rules.' Apparently, they failed, or — consistent with 'The Rules' — they decided not to discuss their experiences with me. If they didn't succeed, the irony is that both of my brothers more closely followed in my father's footsteps than I did. Like the 'Systems Guy' that Dad became, they both pursued careers in chemical engineering, personally patenting a number of life-saving breakthroughs such as applications of sapphire single-crystal substrates for increasing the stability of arterial stents and installation of electro-phosphorescent polymers for high-efficiency light-emitting diodes. In everyday life, this expertise translated to an affinity for one-word answers and the ability to make instantaneous judgments of "you're right" or "you're wrong." In my personal explorations of the nuances of the system, thinking in terms of right and wrong or black or white are not beneficial traits for exploring 'The Rules.' To dissect the code, you needed the utmost appreciation of ambiguity and a reverence for the mystique of insoluble problems.

At first, the calls with Dad were a bit awkward. In the past, Mom sent lengthy hand-written letters, punctuated with her pre-emoji hand-drawn faces expressing various emotions. There was a frequent open-ended phone call, in which Mom would probe to find what was most relevant in our lives, whether you intended to reveal it or not. Might as well fess up at the outset; she's going to get to you no matter how long it takes. She'd always had the mindset of the village griot, precisely recording details of each personal story of all of her flock. Eidetic memory, they call that. Taking a snapshot of the event, and then retrieving each detail as needed. She would, seemingly naively, dredge up details later on to support a particular viewpoint ("Remember that time when Debbie Sutton beat you in that spelling bee?"). Of course, as the consummate storyteller, she'd always introduce distortions and embellishments to make the telling more captivating. *A story is only a good story if the listener is engaged*, she used to say.

After a while, I learned to stop correcting and adjusting her distortions and just listen. *Now that's an interesting interpretation of what happened...* And quite often, her altered version of the story contained a deeper level of understanding of what actually transpired.

During this new era of phone call visits with Dad, I was surprised when he started confiding certain personal things to me. About doubts, hopes, dreams and fantasies, things I had tried to discuss with him for decades, unsuccessfully. He told me that Kate had started inviting him again to "support groups, whatever those are," to help deal with living with "the Mother," as he called her. He asked me if I thought they would help.

"Help?" I asked naively. "Do I think support groups will help? Help you deal with…?"

"Yeah, help," he cut me off. "Help me feel…like I can *do something* about all this."

"Do something? What do you mean by 'do something?' What do you think you can do?"

Journalistic leading questions. Let the subject do all the talking.

I think the effect, however small, of support groups is to demonstrate that sometimes there is *nothing* you can do. And this sense of helplessness inevitably reminds us of times we have been harmed and were unable to do anything to stop the pain. I do believe that if we have been harmed, we have to relive the moment of harm, and we have to confront the harm *as a living being* — real or imagined and decide to respond to it differently from how we responded initially.

I waited for a while. Dad didn't say anything. *No, that's going too far. I pushed him too far. He's clamming up now.*

Changing the topic, I asked Dad how life was without drinking his daily scotch.

"I just want to be *clear*," he said, with a slight tone of regret. "That's why I gave it up."

"Clear?" I echo back. "Clear for what?"

"Don't know exactly. For what happens next." This was new. དྲན་པ།. *Drumpa*. A bit of Zen enlightenment leaking out of my father.

"That's good, Dad. Clear for what's going to happen next. That's all you can do."

I imagined at that moment Dad coming out of a shell. He was shedding some sort of protection. Maybe he was climbing out of the protection that living with Mom had provided him all these years.

6. The Systems Guy

Time is one of the greatest of all human inventions. The Greeks invented a mythology of time as a serpent with three heads. The Egyptians devised a legend of a goddess floating down a river, holding palm branches in each of her hands, each one with endless notches. The Indians proposed a wheel of creation, destruction, and rebirth, rotating in endless repetitions. They all knew that time was essential for experiencing the complexity and the mystery of our lives, but impossible to describe accurately.

I developed my own time construct during my Peace Corps days in Togo. I would sometimes sit alone on weekend evenings at "Café L'Oasis," a local watering hole near my house in Lomé. I would contemplate the notion of 'grammar' — what is it that holds a language together? Perhaps under the influence of *Bière Benin* and an occasional shot of *sodabé*, the local palm wine, I developed what I assumed was an original idea. Eureka! Grammar is verb-based and consists of five layered translucent curtains: tense, modality, aspect, certainty, and voice. Each language — and each person in their own idiolect — accomplishes the trick of expressing the experience of time somewhat differently. Much like the myths of serpents, rivers, and wheels.

I think Dad came up with his own new construct of time in the weeks that followed Mom's diagnosis of Alzheimer's. Previously, each twenty-four-hour day consisted of a sequence of events. Mom and Dad each understood the other's grammar. Dad and Mom had always *planned* for the future — the trips, the get togethers, new items for the house or yard to save for and eventually acquire. Now, Dad was realizing, none of that really mattered.

The most immediate beneficial effect of Mom's diagnosis was that Dad had the opportunity to rethink his relationships. Rethink relationships with his kids, his relatives, his neighbors, his old work colleagues, his old army buddies, waiters at Denny's and clerks in Walgreens. It made him examine how he *felt* about other people, about his ability to reach them if he wanted to. For so long Dad had been an understudy, a role player in Mom's social world, the network of relationships she had built for them as a couple. And now, maybe for the first time, Dad realized he needed to reinvent his own ability to connect with fellow humans.

One thing I learned about Dad early on in my life was that you had to be strategic if you needed something from him. He was 'available' for only a few fleeting moments at a time. If you wanted him to listen to a problem, if you needed an authentic response, an honest answer, his real insight, you had to catch him at those rare moments when he was 'between systems.' That was my term for it. You had to grab him when he wasn't in a programmed mode to get something done. Only then, when he wasn't 'in gear,' could he actually hear what you were saying.

Dad was a military-trained company man, the quintessential systems guy. Like the old saying, "For a man with a hammer, the whole world is a nail." For Dad it was, "For a man with a system, the whole world is a series of chaotic events needing someone to impose order."

So as time went on after The Diagnosis, and the old grammar that held his world together began to collapse, Dad began to learn a new system. First goal: How to communicate with Mom in her 'uncommunicative state.'

Dad learned to say things like "Let me help you with that" rather than "I'll do that for you." Or "I'm sorry that you're upset" rather than, "What's wrong?" At first glance, he just learned to say *something* where he would usually just be silent.

He also learned to craft his non-verbal behavior more carefully: Don't raise your voice. No sudden movements. Don't show alarm. Don't act offended. Don't force her to do something. Don't object. Don't ignore her when she wants something. Don't argue with her even when she's obviously 'wrong,' saying something that contradicts the 'facts.' Don't shame her or criticize her. And a big one: Don't take it personally when she attacks you.

Which she did. Often.

It is hard to weather attacks when there is no end in sight to the barrage. But it can be done. One battle at a time. This is, after all, one of the skills of a patient warrior. Bear the intensity, with dignity, with honor; with expectation of victory, but not with a grasping for that victory.

For Dad, adjusting the system wasn't just a language shift. It was also a transformation of perspective: You have to appreciate that there are multiple codes of operation in the world. Some of the codes have nothing to do with organizational patterns. Some have nothing to do with the truth. And there is room for all of them!

Once Dad saw Mom's new *way* of communicating, as 'a system,' he was able to learn it, to reverse engineer it, to master it.

During his forty years at Ford Motor Company, Dad worked with computer systems. He rarely talked about his work at home, so to us kids 'what our father did' seemed to be: get dressed in a white shirt and tie, stand up straight, look important, show up at your place of work, stay all day and come home.

White collar work seemed like a big scam to me, even at age ten. I used to admire the train conductors, the truck drivers, the cops, the TV repairmen, the milk delivery guys. I knew what they did, and it seemed important.

One day, Dad took me to work at his office at Ford Motor Company, I guess on a 'take your kid to work' day. What I remember most clearly were green metal dividers and glass windows between workspaces, and gray metal desks with chairs on rollers with processions of people walking in and out of these little cubicles, leaving stacks of papers, and giving coded directives. Robot-ville is what I called it. Don't want any part of that. Is it possible to escape from here?

I *thought* Dad made cars. I mean, he drove one and told me that's what he did, "I make cars." This looked like some convoluted scheme to make everyone look important. "Where are all the cars?" I kept asking.

In spite of discovering the conspiracy to hide the actual cars from me, I did gain a degree of respect for Dad that day. He was doing something that seemed to require secret knowledge. It seemed remarkable to me that adults could make up a job like this; one that allowed them to dress up in comical gear and act important, say things like "Honey, I'm home," get a kiss from your wife, and get paid well enough to support a family.

At home, Dad was generally banging away building something; he was a crackerjack carpenter and easily could have made a living at that — something that had endeared him to Grandpa Elias, Mom's father. Elias Hofmann was himself a professional carpenter, a self-made man. Son of German immigrants from Dresden, who supported a family of nine children, building houses that are still standing proud today, including the one Mom grew up in.

Dad would occasionally visit Grandpa Wilhelm to get advice on a carpentry project. And he'd invite Grandpa Wilhelm over to inspect one of his finished projects — a bench, a picnic table, a shelf, a room extension. I don't remember ever hearing Dad and Grandpa Wilhelm have any kind of verbal exchange. Both were men of few words, though it was clear to me that they apparently admired each other's work. They had a nuanced system of non-verbal cues, a subtle nod, a slight cocking of the head, a soft stroking of the hand over a smooth wood surface. They would stand in front of the work of art they were admiring, grunt in unison, and smoke Pall Malls, first tapping the tobacco in place on their brownish thumbnails. *Pat-pat-pat.*

When I got older, Dad finally leaked that his job at Ford was a 'systems analyst.' *Why didn't you say so earlier?* I didn't know what it meant, but it sounded spy-level critical to the future of the planet. He explained that it had something to do with making sure that all of the inventory needed for manufacturing was available at the right time. When I didn't seem to grasp this, he divulged that if just one item was missing — "a bolt, let's say"— the whole process would grind to a halt. And "somebody's head would roll."

Avoiding the 'head roll' seemed like a strong motivation to do your job well. I was gradually learning what I would come to know as "Jake's Rules," including this one: *Keep your job. Stay on the frickin' payroll.*

Dad's belief in 'following the system' was more than just having a set of rules to revert to when needed. It included a pervasive 'faith *in* the system.' Faith gave him a reason to have hope in the future. But now, he felt it, he felt it like a punch in the gut that he had never experienced before: There was a *crack* in the system. At first, he attempted to shrug it off as a test of his *faith* in the system: *You're just being tested, Daniel.*

That didn't work.

Now he wanted more. He wanted to understand 'this,' to grasp what was happening without falling back on beliefs, belief in religion, belief in the system, maybe even belief in 'The Rules.'

7. The Mirror

When I was a kid, I used to sit in my parents' bedroom when my mother got ready for a night out. I thought my mother looked like a movie star whenever she dressed up in her shiny silk dresses, adorned with glitzy jewelry, pursing and contorting her lips as she put on bright red lipstick. She transformed magically into a movie star!

And of course, when she and Dad left for their evening out, wherever they were off to, I held that image of her in my mind. I assumed my mother would *always* look like a movie star, a Jane Russell, a Joan Crawford or a Rita Hayworth in their prime: perfect, glamorous, untouchable, unchanging.

I wasn't prepared for what I was going to encounter during my visit to Mom following her recent diagnosis with Alzheimer's and an introduction to a new drug regime.

As soon as I walked in the front door, still a bit groggy from a day of travel, I saw my mother standing in the kitchen, stooped, shivering. No, this is not Jane Russell… *Who is this? What the hell is going on here? Are you auditioning for a part in Psycho?*

No, this can't be happening!

It couldn't have been more than a couple of months after Mom's diagnosis. I had arranged to stop by after an all-night flight from Brazil, then a connection through Miami to Cincinnati. I was knackered, and probably should have spent a day in Miami to brace myself before entering The Twilight Zone.

My first thought was that I might be hallucinating. Travel does that to me, gives me virtual peyote trips as I traipse through airports and limo rides to hotels. When I close my eyes this time, I still see images of toucans and the merging brown-blue waters of the Amazon. When I open them, I see this. . .woman whom I have known all my life.

Who is this woman? Is this really my mother? She was shriveled, curled inward, shaking, rocking rhythmically from head to toe, leaning, positioned in the corner, like a wilting philodendron that hasn't been watered in months.

Is someone giving her arsenic? I wondered.

I heard that Mom had started on her regimen of prescribed medications a few weeks earlier, and I had imagined: *Ah, miracle drugs! Of course, there are breakthrough drugs for this condition. That will solve everything.*

We might have been standing facing each other for a full minute. Her voice quivered when she finally noticed me over her shoulder, "G-g-gabe? Is tha-a-at you?"

She looks at me, then past me at my portable black suitcase on wheels. Her hand raises from her side, shaking. She's pointing at the suitcase behind me. She looked at the suitcase as if she was possessed by a vision, a Holocaust survivor spotting one of her Auschwitz guards decades later on the streets of New York, eyes bulging from her head. "No, no. Don't bring that in here! Oh, my. What *is* that? That is so big. That's too big for our house. Please take it away. Oh, my. I can't believe how big that is. Take it away now. Oh-oh-oh." She covers her face as if bracing for an imminent attack.

Uh-oh. We're in uncharted territory now. For any communication to work between two people, there has to be 'common ground.' Mutual agreements about time and space, the laws of physics, for instance. For Mom now, time was either moving very fast or extremely slow. Items were either massively large or microscopically tiny. Things were too close or too far. Perspectives shifted constantly. It was hard to agree on anything.

The very ground was shifting for Mom, and her perception of the world she was living in was clearly frightening for her.

Was it the medication? Or was it the disease?

Whatever it was, it was consuming her, eating her up. Sucking blood from the nape of her neck. *Thluuuup, let me suck the life right out of you.*

I don't recall what happened next. Traumatic encounters like this have a way of wiping me out, particularly when coupled with jet lag. Moments later, I was lying down on the couch to rest and I must have dozed off. Overwhelmed. The fatigue of the trip. And the realization that I had now officially and irrevocably 'lost' my mother.

When I awoke and staggered to my feet and looked around to orient myself, I saw Mom standing in the hall bathroom, staring in the mirror.

Why am I so dizzy? Is this jet lag? Maybe I'm seasick? How long have I been out? Where am I? Is this Manaus, the Amazon, the jungle? Why is my mother in Brazil?

Gathering myself, I stood up and walked toward her. *What the hell? She can't be any worse off than I am.* "Hi Mom," I said, standing behind her putting my hands on her shoulders. "Or is that Rita Hayworth?"

She didn't hear me. She only stared blankly into the mirror. "When can I…?" Her voice trailed off.

"What, Mom?" I asked, gripping her shoulders a bit more tightly.

"When can I go home?"

"You are home, Mom," I remind her, stroking her upper arms. "This is your home."

She shook her head. "No, when can I go *home*? To *my* home?"

I imagine the voices in her head, questioning everything, rerouting things she used to know.

She seems to notice me for the first time. She looks startled. "Why are you there? Why are you standing behind me?"

"It's me, Mom. It's Gabe," I said calmly. "I'm here to visit you."

"Oh, you don't want to visit me now," she announced, "not now."

We may have stood there for another minute, in silence. Dyschronometria, the inability to gauge passage of time. We both have it.

Then she looked up at her image. "What is this?" she asked, putting her finger on the glass.

"It's *just* a mirror. That's you and me in the mirror."

"Oh, it's not," she protests. "I see y-y-you, but who is that next to you?"

"That's all right, Mom. It's magic. It shows you all kinds of different things."

I realized I'm a complete beginner at this. Novice, debutante, greenhorn. I had no idea if it was the right thing to say.

She was trembling again, unable to speak.

Maybe she was looking for herself as a young beauty queen, dressed in ruby red, the one who fell in love with a dashing soldier, a hero, just returned from the war.

She teared up.

"Oh, I'm so sad," she says quietly, trembling.

"Sometimes we all get sad," I told her. "It's okay."

"But I don't know anymore."

"Why don't we say a prayer together?" I suggested.

"Oh, okay," she answered, her sniffles subsiding a bit. The code is switching to her native dialect, the one she is most comfortable with.

"How about that prayer to St. Ann?" I offered. "Let's say that."

Now, she's in her element. We repeat the prayer she has said hundreds of times before.

Dear St. Ann, though I am but a prodigal child, I appeal to you and place myself under your great motherly care. Please listen to my prayers… shu-shu-shu…

She recited the prayer, spine straight, shaking gone, with clarity, dignity and grace. Like a movie star, photogenic from every angle, her voice resonant, she finished the soliloquy in just one take.

.

44

8. Admission Day

One Sunday morning, the tipping point came.

"Da-a-a-n, help me…" Mom called from the bed. Dad was at the kitchen table, eating a bowl of Sugar Pops, drinking coffee and reading the *Cincinnati Enquirer*, as he did every morning, an hour or so before Mom woke up.

"I can't move my legs! I forgot how to move my legs,*"* she tells him as he enters the bedroom.

Dad calls Kate right away. S-O-S. "It's your mother. She can't walk." No ambiguity about this message.

Kate is prepared for this.

When she arrives at the house, she explains that Mom needs to be taken to a hospital for evaluation. Now.

Dad of course knew this decision was a foregone conclusion, with his logical Systems-Guy mind, but his emotional mind, his dream mind, was holding on as long as possible.

Then, Kate explains, standing right in front of him: *Are you listening?* "Mom will have to be moved to Ellingwood."

Serendipitously, Ellingwood Retirement Community, with its large blue-and-white wooden sign reading "Your Journey Begins at Ellingwood," is a multi-purpose nursing home very near them, less than a mile away.

Kate explains the conclusion to Dad as a mother would to a child, articulating each word with clear boundaries between them: "This. is. what. we. have. to. do. now.'"

Kate wouldn't need to tell Dad what he already knew: *You have done all that was humanly possible, and now Mom will be in better care.*

It's a hard pill to swallow.

Kate answers the question before he can even ask. "You can visit her every day. You can be there as often as you want."

It's over, Dad thought. *Life as we've known it. Over.*

He looked down at his hands, frozen in time. *Can't we go back and have a re-do?*

The roller coaster ride with Mom at home, on and off various drug regimens, had been continuing for months. At times, there had been optimistic signs. She'd smile at a joke. She'd nod when someone told a story. She'd ask questions. Mom would occasionally appear to enjoy certain things — walking in her garden — if only for a few minutes, chatting with neighbors, looking through picture albums and acknowledging faces — though only for a few page turns. But *any* kind of enjoyment derived from routines or pleasure taken in little activities was to be valued and nurtured.

"Positive affect," that's what they call it in psychology. The extent to which an individual experiences positive moods such as joy, interest, alertness, gratitude.

Positive affect was the cure!

Reports from Kate: She smiled. She laughed. She participated. She joined. She initiated. She shared. She appreciated. She took a walk in the garden today and noticed the petunias in bloom. She laughed at the pictures you sent of Haze — our black Labrador — dressed like a ballerina. She went for an ice cream sundae at Dairy Queen after dinner!

Hearing the news, for a few precious moments, I would think, *She's back. All this nightmare stuff was just an illusion.*

But the inexorable march of the disease would parade back to the forefront. Though there were ongoing flashes of 'the cure,' those moments were in reality only a tiny percentage of her life. Mostly, there was repetition and confusion, discomfort and pain, antagonism and depression. It was becoming very clear that Mom would soon need full-time care.

Kate was seeing this in her daily visits with Mom. Mom would drift off in different parts of the house. She'd start a task, like tidying up a table or folding laundry and quickly abandon it. She'd become easily agitated and critical. Kate pointed these things out to Dad. He'd nod and make a mental note. *Umm-hmm, Umm-hmm,* he'd say under his breath. *But not yet,* he'd say to himself. *Not yet.*

Kate gradually convinced Dad of the benefits of a nursing home. At a nursing home, there would be more possibilities for regular doses of the positive-affect cure. There would be bingo sessions, visits from entertainers, concerts from local school kids, therapy dogs, exercise pools, a crew of young, engaging, humorous, talkative aides.

As one repetitive day bled into another, depression set in for Dad. There was no longer any pretense that Mom would recover in any medical sense. But he maintained the hope that she would be taken care of with dignity until 'the hour' came upon her. No one wanted to talk about that — the *ultimate* conclusion — but that was always on everyone's mind. How will all this end?

When the ambulance comes, the technician knocks gently on the front door. *Tat-tat.* A routine call for the EMR guys. They're being intentionally quiet and cautious — thank God they didn't come with sirens blaring — but they materialize like extraterrestrials. *How did you get here? Who let you in?* Unwelcome.

Mom registers the sound of unfamiliar shuffling on her floors. Foreboding. *Why are you here? Outsiders entering my world.* She understands a major transition is taking place. The *psh-psh-pshing* of Kate and Dad whispering in the background is all part of the conspiracy to whisk her away.

Mom bites hard on her lower lip in protest, as two white-clad technicians enter the hallway and gravitate toward her bedroom. With an air of authority, they efficiently move Mom from her bed onto a gurney. She can only vaguely register the sensations of people handling her body. *Is this my body? Where are my legs?* The words she hears sound like growling German phrases from her childhood. *Tun Sie das, dass.*

Dad is now somehow restored to his role as problem-solver. He places a hand on her chest to calm her. "You'll be all right, Ems. You'll be all right." She looks up at him with terror in her eyes. *How can I believe you?*

Dad turns his attention to the paramedics. "Watch her legs. Careful with her back. Slowly. Easy now." *Why can't you do this more soothingly?*

"I can't believe you're *doing* this to me!" Mom growls harshly, as the gurney passes the prayer room and the paramedics jostle the gurney to get it through the front door.

You've taken away my bridge game, my cooking, my movement, and now my prayer room! What else can you take from me?

They guide the gurney to the back of the white, blocky ambulance waiting in the driveway. It is an ugly, ugly vehicle, she notes, massive and scarred. It's waiting to take her away.

How did that get here? It's so big!

Kate sidles up next to Mom in the back of the van. The ambulance door closes with a conclusive imperious thud. One of the technicians shakes Dad's hand warmly and says, "we'll take care of her, sir."

He nimbly slides into the driver's seat. The van pulls away from the driveway.

And then Dad practices his new skill, crying. His heart is broken.

For once in his life, he is not sure what will happen next. But whatever it is, he knows he will be there for it.

Part Two: Listening

The Visit

The Castle Gardens

The Perfect Game

Leonardo

The Field Trip

The GABA Gene

The Inheritance

The Protection Code

The Secret

50

9. The Visit

My earliest memories of television were lying on the living room floor, watching game shows like *Twenty-One* and *The $64,000 Question*. My mother and father used to schedule around the air times of these shows, devouring them religiously and of course, playing along with the contestants, competing with each other. I could imagine that my mother would be a formidable opponent in whatever undertaking she chose — sports, academics, or game shows. I remember her leaning forward in her chair, ready to pounce on the next question. Then the whoops of victory when she got the answer right. *Whoo-hoo!*

I remember marveling at how much my parents knew! Geographic sites, historical facts, origins of theories. *Where did you learn all this...stuff?*

I later learned that these game shows were rigged. Apparently, the sponsors of the show, like Geritol, were quite unhappy when they saw a legitimate version of the quiz show, *Twenty-One*. They felt the contestants were making a mockery of the show format by revealing how little they actually knew. "You mean, this is all that an average human knows?!" What's the entertainment value in that?

Apparently, to appease the angry public outcry, the shows were all cancelled. But eventually, they were replaced by lower-stakes games in the early 1960s, particularly *Jeopardy.*

I still think they're rigged. But that's okay. It's good entertainment, the constant self-examination, the incessant quizzing.

I think Dad may have watched every episode of *Jeopardy* since its inception. Alex Trebek was everywhere in our house it seemed, a regular feature of our lives, testing us, testing us. *Try this one. What is the name for...?*

Through the open screen door, I hear Alex whisper the test item from the TV in the living room in his reflective hushed tone. "The group Nazareth took its name from the first line of a 1968 song by *this* group..."

Wait, don't tell me, I know this... Nazareth, Nazareth...Damn, it's on the tip of my tongue. The third sin of memory, blocking, a temporary inaccessibility of stored information. *Forgot the access code!*

Tap, tap. I cause the screen door to vibrate rhythmically.

Through the screen, I can see Dad inside, but I don't want to startle him.

I imagine that he's going to be happy to see me. It's my first visit to him since Mom has been admitted to Ellingwood, the first time ever I will be visiting him, at his house, without my mother being there.

He doesn't hear me. I tap again with the back of my knuckles. A mild vibration passes up my arm. Autonomous sensory meridian response. Paresthesia. See, I too can find ways to entertain myself.

"Hi, Dad. It's me." I call above the sound of *Jeopardy*. He can't hear me. I decide to ring the bell.

Ding-dong.

That did the trick. There's a pause while he decides if the sound is coming from the TV or from somewhere else.

"Who the hell is that?" he says, seemingly to himself, but loud enough for the intruder to hear.

He lowers the volume and I hear Alex as he undertones the answer to his last clue — "The Band" — with a veiled message to the players — and the audience. *"You're all idiots if you didn't know this."* Then he gives the answer we should have known all along: "The song was called *The Weight*."

Boy, you're going to carry that weight, carry that weight, a long time. Of course! The Weight.

"Marcie, you're up…" Alex says forgivingly, with a tone of "Let's see if you fools can get this one right." He never lets on that he has read all of the questions and answers in preparation for today's show.

The contestant selects the next clue, "I'll take *Rock Bands* for twelve hundred."

Dad approaches the door. "Yeah?" I'm glad Dad became something of a pacifist after the war. His growl is just a kind of aposematism, a warning sign to keep predators away.

I brace for the kind of outburst I've seen him dish out to strangers who have misguidedly intruded on him. He squints through the screen. "Oh, Gabe, is that you?" His voice has calmed. Ah, I can exhale now.

"Hi, Dad," I say. This entire transaction has taken a full minute at least, as if we were acting in a sea of molasses. Welcome to the world of protracted motion. Is this dissociative disorder? Or dyschronometria? Or a dorsolateral brain lesion? Or is this simply just getting old?

"What the hell are you doing here?" Dad says as he opens the door slowly to let me in.

"What am I doing?" I decide to pick up the pace. "Selling Girl Scout cookies! This year we have *Caramel Delites* and *Savannah Shout-Outs*," I mime, holding up my backpack like a shopping bag. "Can I put you down for a dozen of each?"

That did the trick. Woke him up. *Witzkampf.* A battle of wits. Crafting a comeback. Dad loves verbal play. He smiles.

"No, I'm here to visit you, remember? One week in paradise with my dear old Dad."

I'm keeping things light, but I can see he's upset. I can tell the arrangement of my visit has slipped his mind. The first sin of memory, transience. Anything novel, not part of a pattern, is likely to be forgotten.

Now I can sense from just a few moments with him that he has become a different person, a bit slower, more deliberate, a bit more reclusive.

He's obviously rattled he didn't remember. I try to mitigate his embarrassment. "I'm sorry. I…"

"No, th…that's okay," he stutters, massaging his lower lip with his first two fingers.

I continue to apologize for the intrusion. "I should have called you from the airport. Sorry, I was in a rush. I had to catch the bus to the rental car lot, slipped my mind."

"Well, come on in. The guest room is all yours." He holds the door open wider, a matador extending his cape. *Come this way, no escape, you're mine now.*

I schlep my bag from the porch and move it inside, sliding it toward the stairs leading down to the basement.

"Oh, do you have a rental car?" he asks quizzically, as I set down my bag.

I recognize from the tone of his voice that this is a coded message. Like most men from the G.I. Generation, Dad uses cars as a symbol of identity, individuality, independence, strength…the list never ends.

I turn around to face him. *"A Hyundai Elantra."* I can see the disappointment on his face. "Sorry, they were all out of Fords."

He grins to acknowledge my continuance of our *Treppenwitz* exchange. Dad was a lifer at Ford, a systems analyst from the early computer days. Ford gave him his life, really. His steady work landed him a nice promotion when I was in my early teen years, moving us out of his Ohio plant job to the big time in Detroit.

As an act of reverence for his Maker, he insisted that all of his children — and anyone who wished to be called his friend for that matter — declare loyalty to the Ford brand.

"Did you park it on the right edge of the driveway?" he asks, suddenly very serious.

Wow, this gambit in the *Treppenwitz* match surprises me. I'm not sure what he means by this.

Dad has always had a set of puzzling rules for visitors — regulations about setting the thermostat, locking doors, cleaning dishes, not touching his pile of papers on his worktable. My guess was he'd ratcheted the house policies up a notch once Mom was admitted to Ellingwood. He wanted to maintain order. I decided not to ask the reason for this new parking statute.

"Can I do that later?" I ask. I realize right away this challenge was a mistaken strike at the system. Not the right calculation on my part. I see him go into 'systems mode.'

"No, I'd rather you do it now. You never know when…" he trails off. "No problemo."

I most certainly don't want to start this visit out with any friction over The Rules.

I go back outside and reposition the Elantra precisely six inches from the edge of the lawn.

Closing the car door and locking it with the remote — *buu-bup* — it dawns on me. Dad wants me to leave space in case he needs to back his car out of the garage, which is always parked on the left side.

Maybe he thinks Ellingwood might call in the middle of the night — an emergency. *Mr. Bron, you need to come over right away. Your wife is...*

By the time I get back into the house, Dad is already back in front of the TV in his chair, feet up, watching *Jeopardy*. They're in the *Double Jeopardy* phase of the match now. Marcie is in the lead. "I'll take Signs and Symbols for one thousand please..." Alex intones the next exam item, inviting all due respect that he has already divined the answer: "Meant to evoke a person with arms outstretched and pointed downward, it was designed in 1958 by Gerald Holtom..."

I take my stuff downstairs to the bedroom. "What is the peace sign?" I say to myself, as I descend the steps. *Bing-bing-bing!* When I'm in Dad's house, I tend to go immediately into game mode.

Is this a survival tactic? That I need to entertain myself by engaging in games?

I plop my bag next to the dresser. The guest room looks exactly like it did the last time I was here a couple of months ago. The green shag carpeting. The extensive network of desks and counter space and shelving, with cutesy knick-knacks and framed photographs. The sagging double bed, which must be the original bed that Dad and Mom owned, covered with a worn-out pink, flowered nylon spread.

Still in game mode, I close my eyes to test myself, to see if I can visualize and name all of the items in the room. I use the 'Memory Palace' technique, placing each object in a sequence of rooms in my childhood home. It's going to be a long week — games galore.

10. *The Castle Gardens*

It looks like I have been kicked out of my yoga class. I'm wearing a scarlet red loin cloth, nothing else. I was kicked out by Lakshmi, the teacher. She claimed that I was criticizing her teaching style, but all I did was make some suggestions for improving. If only you would speak a bit less... Out! She shouted, pointing to the door.

Now that I've been banished and that I have no yoga teacher, I walk outside the class searching for a new teacher and notice for the first time that the classroom has transparent glass walls. No doors, I can't go back in even if I want to.

So, turning away, I am now on a green hillside. As I walk, I see that a massive factory has just let out and a large group of workers, with hard hats and lunch pails, are all walking toward me. After a moment, I notice a very attractive woman in the middle of the group. I recognize her! It's Yamamoto-sensei, one of my first yoga teachers, from Japan. She is also dressed in red. She emerges from the crowd and walks toward me. I tell her how beautiful she looks. She blushes and looks down at the ground modestly.

I now notice that she is wearing a modern, expensive red business suit with high-heeled leather shoes, quite unlike the usual simple all-black yoga attire and bare feet, as I remember her from the last time I saw her, years earlier.

She still hasn't spoken yet, and beckons me toward a bookstore, where somehow, she directs me toward a display of cookbooks. I don't know where to begin exploring, so she helps me sort quickly through the enormous pile of books, and I extract one that I sense is the one I should have. I don't need the entire book, she indicates, so I tear out the single page she has specified and bring it with me.

I follow her to a valley among the green hills where she instructs me that we are to begin. "Begin what?" I ask. I am to prepare her as a meal, she tells me. Say that again, please. You'll understand, she indicates with her eyes, looking down at the ground, all lush green grass.

She removes her clothes and I see now that Yamamoto-sensei is my mother, as she was at that age. Her skin, surprisingly, is white and pale, like a plucked chicken, watery and splotchy and bumpy, not the idyllic smooth, alluring skin I had imagined her to have under her clothes.

I hesitate, silently hoping for a way out of this task, but I know that what she is directing me to do is very important. She reassures me it is okay. Okay? Okay to be with me. Okay to "take me apart." I am tearful, as

I really do not want to do this. But I am proceeding as she is instructing me, silently, reluctantly, but knowing this is something I am destined to do.

I take a knife and begin to separate her into parts, as she guides me through this process. Soon she is entirely dismembered, but her consciousness remains fully in each of her parts, glowing out like sunlight, and communicating with me. Telling me I am doing the right thing.

Suddenly, we see a two-dimensional cartoon character, who looks like Moe, the grouchy, penurious, violent-tempered bartender from the Simpsons, lurching over one of the hills in our direction, vaulting quickly toward us as if bouncing on springs. She says, uh-oh, he isn't going to be happy when he sees me like this. Indeed, as the man's face comes into view, I see he is irate. But it's not a cartoon character anymore. It's my father. He is upset that she has allowed me to see her like this. I fear that he is going to tear me apart.

I awaken, in the guest room of Dad and Mom's house. Damn! What was that all about? It's vague: Yamamoto-sensei, my first teacher, dressed in red, the color of energy, danger, strength, power, passion; a bookstore, the font of knowledge and inspiration; a dissection, peeling away, trying to get at the heart of something; glowing light, providing guidance. Okay, that's all good. But who the hell is Moe, the two-dimensional bartender who was about to *tear me limb from limb*? Feelings of being cut off, disempowered, or isolated. Experiencing a significant loss. A loss of power, abilities, or identity.

Why me? Do I really have to go through this? Can't I just forgo the dreams and get on with things? Can't I just prepare to have a normal visit with my mother?

Shortly after breakfast, I am at Ellingwood, visiting Mom. I arrive at the entry station, the portal into this parallel universe, acting as if I've been here many times before. I go through the ritual of signing in, showing ID, marking my entry time, indicating who I will be visiting.

Everyone is cheerful as I walk toward Room 103 where Mom is staying, but I have an overriding anticipation that I will be hearing the clanking of jail cell doors closing behind me.

She sees me as soon as I enter. She's been eyeing the door apparently, waiting to pounce.

"Get me *out* of here!" is the first thing she says to me, under her breath and barely moving her lips, to avoid being detected by the guards.

It's my first visit to see Mom since she transitioned to Ellingwood, and already she's recruiting me for an escape.

Mom has been here for a month. I imagine the first weeks were rife with escape plots whenever Dad and Kate came to visit.

Here's the plan. We're going to dig three separate tunnels, Tom, Dick, and Harry. So if Fritz is onto one of them, we close it down and still have two other routes out.

The first thing I notice about Mom is that she's gained weight. I guess they stopped the arsenic-laced diet. She has also regained a bit of her former glow. Maybe they've found the right dose of meds. There's hope!

I try humor to evade getting involved in the escape plot: "Mom, you really don't want to leave. They haven't even had the Miss Ellingwood pageant this year — and I'm sure you'll want to enter."

She grits her teeth: "Don't try to humor me," she says. "This place is awwwwwful." She draws out the low "aw" sound, in a practiced German guttural growl, to be sure I understand her.

I ask her if she'd like to give me a tour of the place. She frowns again. "Oh, I see what you're doing. You're going to try to convince me. Show me how nice everything is."

"Oh, you're onto me, Mom. But can you show me around?"

I move behind her wheelchair and push her out into the hallway and toward the atrium in the middle of the building.

We pause in front of the glass, where there are a number of colorful birds. We watch them for a while, no more than a few minutes, and then she turns around in her wheelchair.

"Oh, Gabe, how good to see you!" She smiles cheerfully.

Here we go. I've been preparing for this. Dr. Alvarez, the neurologist on duty at Ellingwood, recently declared that Mom is now firmly in Stage 2 Alzheimer's:

- Forgetting events that happened just moments earlier.
- Being forgetful of events or personal history.

- Feeling moody or withdrawn, especially in socially or mentally challenging situations.
- Being unable to recall information about herself like her address or telephone number, and the high school or college she attended.
- Experiencing confusion about where she is or what day it is.
- Demonstrating personality and behavioral changes, including suspiciousness and delusions or compulsive, repetitive behavior like hand-wringing or tissue shredding.

"Hi, Mom." I lean down to kiss her forehead.

I can get used to this, just living in the present tense. No more hypotaxis, embedding events within other events, no precedents, no conclusions. Now it's all parataxis: this happens, then this happens, then this. That's all there is.

"Where are you staying?" she asks.

"I'm staying at your house," I say automatically, then quickly correct myself. "I'm staying with Dad."

She doesn't notice my slip and self-correction. "Are you getting enough to eat at Dad's?"

"Yes, Mom," I say.

Actually, I'm lying about this. Dad has virtually nothing to eat at the house, except for snacks and frozen dinners, and I haven't yet had time to make a run to Kroger's.

Feeding people well was always something Mom prided herself on. She would *always* make sure that her guests had enough to eat.

"But he's not a good cook!" she protests, pointing out one of Dad's glaring deficiencies. Persistence of memory.

I pause for a bit, trying to decipher where this is all going.

"No, you're right. He's a terrible cook," I confirm. I lean forward to whisper, "All he has is salami and cheese. He eats worse than a college kid in a dorm room. I have to smuggle in fruits and vegetables."

She nods knowingly. She doesn't understand most of the words I'm saying, I realize. Blocking, the third sin of memory. But she knows that she knows them, and I can tell that she doesn't want me to simplify anything for her. I feel that she's trying to come to his defense, "Bu, bu, but, he, he's..."

"It's a very risky business," I continue in a whisper. "When I go out to the supermarket, I don't want him to catch me. It would hurt his feelings."

She smiles at this little espionage game.

Slight pause. But then she reactivates her train of thought. Persistence is the last sin to go.

"I worry that you're not getting anything to eat. He d-doesn't have anything f-f-for you to eat." Her voice is now laced with that telling quiver that means she's getting tired. We'd better get to the garden before she wants to go back to her room.

I pull up a chair from the card table and sit down.

"That's your job, isn't it?" I say, taking her hands in mine. "You are the Worrier. I think there's even a Tarot Card named after you. Emma, the Worrier."

She smiles, knowing that I'm playing with her. "You know what they say in Japanese?" I ask.

She shakes her head left to right, kind of an amused-puzzled gesture.

One piece of advice Howard, the nurse, gave me is: Avoid asking questions. That just reminds the patient that she has a faulty memory. But with Mom, she knows that questions are part of the whole conversational gambit: Pose a question — answer it yourself. She used to do it masterfully. Have to keep the art alive.

"Shinpai shite arigato," I say slowly.

"But I don't know what that m-m-means," she whispers.

"It means, 'Thank you for worrying about me.' People in Japan say it all the time," I tell her.

One of the intriguing things about Japanese communication is the sense of obligation and imposition that people tune into with *every* utterance. *Do you understand what I mean? I'm sorry if I said that too bluntly. I can say it in a different way, if you prefer. Sorry for making you go to so much effort to understand what I'm trying to say. I'm sorry, I'm really sorry, to make you worry so much about me.*

But Mom doesn't recall anything about Japan right now. "I've never been to Japan," she informs me.

"Sure you have," I remind her. "You've visited us lots of times. You loved Japan."

She did love Japan. She liked being out in the streets, experiencing the hustle and bustle of the crowds whirling past. And she could engage people easily, clerks in shops, passengers on trains. Sometimes hold a person in a lengthy conversation. All without speaking a word of Japanese. A miracle of cross-linguistic communication. "Oh, he was such a nice man!" she'd say later about a stranger she'd struck up a conversation with.

Now, Mom's face suddenly clouds with anxiety. "Do you live in Japan?" she wants to know.

"Not anymore, but we used to live there," I say. She looks comforted. I pull out my phone to bring up some pictures, but I can see that her mind has traveled elsewhere. And she doesn't really like digital pictures: Everything looks the same to me, she'd say.

End of that episode.

"Where are you staying now?" she asks, reintroducing a perpetual theme.

"I'm staying at Dad's house."

I *get* the grammar here. We're repeating exchanges, gambits, plays, routines, jams, riffs — just like musicians do, like singers do, just like athletes do, just like actors do. Just like reading the same bedtime stories to my sons when they were little, over and over, each time fresh and new.

"But he doesn't have anything for you to eat," she reminds me, more apologetically than before.

"Thank you for worrying about me," I say. "*Shinpai shite arigato.*"

She smiles. She doesn't remember what it means or why I'm bringing it up, but she knows that it means something and that I have some reason for saying it. That's all that matters.

I change the subject. "This is my first visit here," I say, with upbeat intonation. "Can you show me around?"

"Oh, no. I can't walk," she says sadly. She looks up at me with a quizzical look, as if she's not sure I really understand what's going on.

"That's why they put me here, because I can't walk," she explains to me. I wish I could tell her that it's not her fault, that it's not cause and effect, that we didn't put her here because she couldn't walk.

But that's hypotaxis, embedding reasons and hypotheticals and negatives. Too painful to process all of that.

"Well, tell you what, I'll push your chair," I offer. "But you tell me where to go." Simple sentences. Paratactic organization. This… then this… then this. Easier to follow.

I stand and position myself behind her chair.

"Why don't we go to the garden first?" I suggest. "They say there's a beautiful garden here."

I give the chair a nudge to gain some momentum. *Mgghmmm.* More work than I imagined. We head out toward the garden.

Mom looks upward and back at me over her shoulder, confirming once more who is pushing her forward.

"I know, Mom. Let's play a game," I suggest. "You're the queen and you're showing me around your castle gardens."

"Oh, you boys," she says, mimicking the voice she used so many times to mildly 'scold' me and my brothers when we played tricks on her.

So, it's come to this. My communication with my mother will be coded in secret languages, snippets of encrypted sounds, parsing out pieces of our shared history, with the rules made up as we go along. 'A rogue grammar,' as they call this in linguistics.

Or maybe we don't need a grammar or a language at all, just an understanding. She raises her hand, signaling for me to stop, almost a queen-like gesture to her handlers. She points to a bed of purple prickly flowers to the left.

"Those are bee-b… bee-b… Oh, I don't know what they're called."

"I don't either," I say. "But they're very beautiful."

11. The Perfect Game

One thing that I learned from my father was that victory washes away pain. Now I know that a lot of kids, especially boys, learn that from their fathers and many learn it through sports. The particular flavor of my lesson came from an injury I sustained while playing VYO ("Valley Youth Organization") baseball when I was ten years old.

I was playing second base and running to catch a pop up in shallow right field, tracking the arc of the ball over my shoulder, as I had practiced so many times. Tracking, tracking, seeing it land in my... when 'BAM!' I felt like I hit a brick wall. Apparently, I collided with the right fielder, Eddie Schumaker, who was running full steam from his position, tracking the ball in the opposite direction. I remember a kind of grinding sensation — I collapsed onto the field in a lifeless heap. The two of us were lying on the outfield grass in a daze for what seemed like several minutes before Dad and Mr. Gillinwater, the two team coaches, came out to check on us.

After sitting up for a few minutes, it appeared that the only tangible damage to me was a scraped and bleeding elbow. Somehow, Eddie had similarly little physical damage. Dad grabbed me by the wrists and pulled me up to a standing position. *Good effort, good effort.*

Way to hustle for that ball. That's taking one for the team. You'll be fine. OK, let's go. Two outs. Get your head back in the game here. Let's get this next guy.

Dad also slaps Marty Becker, our centerfielder, on the back, congratulating him for making the play, the play that Eddie and I flubbed. *Head's up play, Marty. That's a live ball, got to play it.* He claps his hands, cheering the troops on, as he jogs back to our bench.

I somehow played the rest of the game in a daze, striking out in my next two at-bats, literally unable to see the ball.

We won the game, though, and I remember celebrating with the team in Mel's Pony Keg, the kids drinking cokes while the coaches drank beer (actually, win or lose, this was our customary post-game ritual). I learned that day about some of the "rules" Dad taught. *Always be ready to take one for the team.* And of course: *Never complain about an injury*, particularly one you've earned in the line of duty. Victory washes away the pain, he reminded me, as he took a final sip of his beer.

I relive this little baseball-is-life lesson as I enter the house, hearing Dad watching a baseball game on TV. I've just come back after visiting Mom.

"Wanna watch the game?" Dad asks, without any debriefing about my visit.

I'm drained. I don't want to watch baseball.

Ah, now I get it. Maybe Dad has forgotten where I was just now. Maybe he's forgotten that this first visit to see Mom in a nursing home would be hard on me.

Or maybe he has thought about all of this, and he knows that watching baseball *is* the best way for us to relieve all of the confusing emotion.

I pour myself a glass of Diet Coke out of the giant urn in the refrigerator into one of the massive blue cups on the counter and join Dad in the living room. He's seated in his customary La-Z-Boy chair, with the remote in his right hand in a ready position.

I plop down on the couch across from his chair and we watch baseball, the familiar voices of announcers, Marty Brennaman and Joe Nuxhall affectionately choreographing every play: "Phillips steps on the bag, pirouettes and fires to first. Oh, it's in the dirt, Perez can't scoop it up. Runner going to second, runner from second is going to score. It's four-nothing Pirates."

There is a kind of soothing poetry in their voices, I note, rich with cadences reminiscent of Hindustani ragas.

"Look at these clowns!" Dad cries out, jolting me out of my reverie. "Can't even turn a routine double play."

It all feels familiar, *déjà vu*. A typical visit with Dad, sitting in front of the TV, making comments, judgments, citing errors.

We sip Diet Coke from large blue Polypro cups, and eat miniature pretzels, scooping handfuls of broken bits from chipped brown plastic bowls, and we watch baseball. We don't say much.

I notice Dad is simultaneously doing a word puzzle of some sort, pausing occasionally to look up into his brow, and chewing the eraser on the end of his pencil. I think for a moment he doesn't even know I'm there, but if I avert my eyes from the TV, he'll give me that 'Is something wrong?' look.

There is something calming about baseball. There is something affirming about baseball. Baseball speaks to you: *There's nothing else you need to be doing.*

When I was a kid, Dad took me and my two brothers to Reds' games regularly during the summer. He'd come home from work around 5:30, flash a smile, and say, "I've got tickets." Sometimes it was four tickets, sometimes just two or three. He was always fair — at least to the boys — remembering whose turn it was to go: Liam's, Gabe's or Theo's.

I never questioned who the opponent was, I just wanted to go to any game. I remember jumping into the back seat of Dad's tan Ford Falcon and leaning out the window like a puppy, ears flapping in the evening breeze, as we approached Crosley Field. To climb the endless concrete steps and eventually see that groomed green grass, golden infield and the fire-engine red seats in a 360-degree panoramic view around the field — it was as ecstatic as any ancient religious ritual must have been to the unwitting masses.

I always brought my tan Rawlings GJ99 baseball glove to the game, hoping to snare a foul ball. I'm not even sure if I ever cared about the score, though Dad did try to teach me how to mark a score card correctly, with all of the little symbols and numbers and special notations, like E-1 for error by the pitcher, E-2 for error by the catcher, E-3 for error by the first baseman, E-4 for error by the second baseman, and so on. A secret code for interpreting the game. For recording it precisely as it happened.

I do remember needing to be shaken out of my reverie when the game was over and it was time to go home. But just having a glimpse of my heroes in person — Frank Robinson, Vada Pinson, Johnny Edwards, Pete Rose — picking up any secret patterns in their attitudes or magical tics in their behavior, made life worth living.

And we saw some of the great ones play The Game: Hank Aaron, Willie Mays, Ernie Banks, Roberto Clemente, Maury Wills. Dad even once corralled the three of us on a school night in September over Mom's protests, to see a game with the Cardinals. "It's Stan Musial's last year — It's his swan song. They've got to see him once in person before they die," Dad insisted.

The child bucket list. I felt so important piling into that station wagon to see 'Stan Music' one last time.

The star players would always do *something* spectacular at every game — a leaping catch, a timely hit, a brilliant piece of base running, an artistic slide. One superhuman play in a three-hour game could make your jaw drop: the rest of the time they were just normal players. "That's what makes them great," Dad said. "They seize the moment. They *always* find a way to impact the game."

I'm about to give up trying to connect with Dad about the visit to Mom. I'll indulge in another round of baseball memories instead.

I ask him, "Do you remember taking Liam, Theo and me to the Reds games at Crosley Field?"

"What?" he asks, alarmed that I've broken the bond of silence we've established these past few minutes. I repeat the question: "Do you remember going to all those games at Crosley Field?"

He shrugs. "That was a long time ago," he says. "They don't even play there anymore."

"Hmm, yeah, I know, but it was a good memory." He's silent, chewing on a new handful of pretzels. "By the way, I saw Mom today."

"Oh, that's where you were," he says.

I do a double take, then realize that it's slipped his mind that I'm visiting him, that I'm here to see Mom, that I've been at the nursing home this afternoon. Transience, the first sin of memory.

I decide to update him on Mom's condition. "Yeah, it was a real…" He cuts me off. "Can we talk about it later, after the game?"

"Sure," I say. "Sure. Let's talk later."

I lean back and exhale deeply. It feels good to let go, to catch on to the drift of the game — what inning, what score, what mood each team is exuding.

The flow of the game, a slightly shifting mantra, has a way of putting things into perspective.

"Let's watch the game. There's nothing else we need to be doing right now."

12. *Leonardo*

I arrive at the Miami airport, on a special mission. My mission is to tame snakes. Not so challenging you may think, but these are invisible snakes. My mission is to tame undetectable snakes, to render them harmless, to make them subservient to human masters.

Poisonous invisible snakes. All kinds: Black Mambas, Indian Cobra (naja naja), Western Diamondback, Timbler Rattlers. I know them all by their real names: Crotalus horridus. Bothrops orphryomegas. Sistrurus ravus. Their real names make them sound like horrible monsters, but any professional snake tamers will tell you that to interact with snakes you have to be dispassionate and see them without loathing, distortion or bias.

I have a reputation in my field, but it is not spotless. I am considered one of the absolute best in my field, but I am not always successful. In fact, I have been killed numerous times by the snakes. But I am always able to regenerate myself. I know the nature of snakes, why they kill, what killing means to them. You control a snake not by confronting it or by trying to end its life, but only by altering its vibration. You can't fool them with visual trickery and certainly you can't outrun them, and oh so naïve of you if you believe you can hide from them. You most certainly cannot deceive them with words.

They know I am coming. They will be infinitely patient and conniving — it's not their fault, that is their nature — and certainly they will outnumber me. They will be trying to find a way to kill me once and for all.

I'm startled awake. I sit up on the edge of the bed, still in darkness, not knowing what time it is. I hear some clattering around in the kitchen on the main floor, so I know Dad is up and into his routine.

I've only been at Dad's house for a few days, and one little disruption I'm noticing is the effect of time distortion. The main aberration in my schedule is that I'm sleeping longer. And very deeply. Very deeply, as in coma-like. Maybe that's a good thing. Maybe I need the rest. Maybe I need the psychic cleansing of dreams. And it's also the dungeon-like feel of the guest room, down in the chilly basement, built into a hillside so there is little natural light. Perpetual darkness, easing me into the underworld of shadows. A by-product of the deep, seemingly endless sleep is that I'm dreaming very vivid dreams.

I slip into a pair of U-M shorts, slip on my orange 'Red Dirt' shirt, and pull on my running shoes. I pop up the stairs, still thinking of how special I am that I know how to change the vibration of snakes. *Who would have thunk it – he knows how to change the vibration of snakes? A superpower!*

As I reach the top of the stairs, I notice the real temperature of the world — it's freaking hot! A steamy southern Ohio morning in summer. And the brightness of the azure blue sky is overwhelming, coming in from the living room window.

I'm starting to head out for Sharon Woods, intending to do a full lap around the lake – about three miles – before breakfast. That's another change in my routine. I normally don't run this much, but I take it upon myself to wear myself out, so I've decided to do a full lap every day.

Before I get to the top of the stairs, I hear him in the kitchen, whistling a tune. It sounds like Paul Simon's *Me and Julio Down By The Schoolyard.*

Dad has always had a habit of idle whistling while tending to his daily chores.

"I'm going out for a run, Dad," I say as I pass him, leaning over the counter. I see that he's making a cup of his instant coffee. I cringe as I imagine the boggy flavor. I've never been able to persuade Dad to go with fresh-brewed — "not worth the trouble," he says. I know it's not polite to leave so quickly, that I should sit down and chat for a while. But I know that once we start talking, I'll lose my chance to get in my run. I'm not motivated enough to get re-energized again.

He gives me a puzzled look, as he stirs his cup — almost as if to say, *Who the hell are you and how did you get here?*

I crouch down to give my shoestrings a final tighten before I head out the door.

"Wait, before you leave, I have a question," he blurts out.

I wonder if this is going to be something serious: he's thinking about the future?

"You're a linguist, right?" he says, sliding back into his chair and picking up his newspaper crossword puzzle.

Oh, okay, got it. He's never shown much interest in my career in linguistics, but at least I *might* be good for solving a crossword clue for him.

"What is the Sanskrit term for… pilgrimage?"

"Hmmm," I mutter. "Pilgrimage? That's a tough one." I had studied ancient languages as part of my training, but not making any connections here.

"Who the hell *speaks* Sanskrit anyway?"

"Nobody," I say. "But it's the mother of all Indo-European languages."

He looks up, with his distinctive 'don't try to impress me, pipsqueak' scowl — a bit softened with age, but still a scowl.

"Well, do you know or not?" he challenges.

"Any clues, like first letter or any vowels?"

"Begins with R, ends with A…nine letters."

"R…ra…ra…a…a…a…Rasa Yatra," I blurt out, not sure where the answer came from. "Does that work?"

He's busy with his pencil, entering the letters. "Yeah, that must be it."

No thank you. No gasps of "how brilliant you are!" Just doing my job, channeling archaic languages for my father.

"Okay, good. Well, I'm out of here." I turn to the door to start my run.

In less than an hour I'm back at the house.

Kreeeeeeen. Ku-cluk-cluk-cluk.

I have always loved the clattering, reverberating sound of a screen door slamming shut. Summertime.

"Paw, I'm home," I announce, bouncing into the kitchen, invoking my inner Opie, southern charm.

Phooo-phooo-phoooo. Deep inhales, deep exhales. Usain Bolt back from his morning training session.

I go into the kitchen and open the refrigerator and grab the bottle of orange juice. Seeing that Dad's not looking at me to express any disapproval, I drink directly from the bottle. I close the refrigerator door with my knee.

I'm in a good mood after my run, having now digested my dream (it's about accepting your challenges and not being afraid of death, I decide) and I'm ready to spar with the champ.

Dad is sitting at the table. He seems to be sketching something. "Where were you?" Dad asks. "I was worried."

I'm still breathing heavily. *"I went for a run in the woods, I told you. Working on a four-minute mile in ninety-nine percent humidity."*

One of the joys of visiting Mom and Dad is a morning jog through Sharon Woods, around the lake, four point seven miles. In the summer it is already steamy by 7:00 a.m., but the asphalt path around the lake, up and down through a myriad of inlets, is still virtually deserted, making it a majestic communing with nature.

"It's so steamy out today*,"* I say, flapping the front panel of my Red Dirt Maui T-shirt, now soaked to a pumpkin orange shade with my sweat. "Already starting to rain a bit."

Dad looks serious. He wants to continue his 'worry conversation.' "Do you have your phone with you?" he asks.

"No, I never take my phone when I run. I'd just lose it."

"Well, you *should*," he says, sliding into a familiar lecturing mode. "I was trying to call you."

Call me? Why? "Oh, sorry," I respond, hoping this will end the exchange.

I can see he's still worried.

"You know, wha-what if…" he stutters. Then he blurts out, "What if something *happened* to you?"

"Happened to me?"

"Yeah, what if something happened to you?" Dad asks, in a challenging voice. "How would they know who you are?"

Now I see it clearly. This is persistence of memory: something bad must have happened in the past… Ah, yes, maybe the time in high school, after we had moved to Michigan, during the Detroit riots, when I came home at three in the morning after a concert and he was up waiting for me, pacing, pacing. Or when…or when… or when. It could have been any one of a number of traumatic experiences that Dad had, as a father, as a soldier, who knows?

I get a glass from the cupboard and pour it full of orange juice. A healthy heart rate is a wonderful thing.

Ah hah! It hits me. It's more than just lingering stress. "Do you mean: if I *die* while I'm running, how will they know who I am?" I ask.

I know "die" is a bit harsh, but I decide to try to take the veil off the conversation. All thinking around trauma, real or imagined, is related to dying, isn't it?

He pauses. "Well, yeah, *something* like that."

I see. This is not just a transgression of a rule — must have phone with you at all times — it's something else. It's something more fundamental.

Ah hah. I think maybe it's time to have 'The Talk' now — the one in which I expound on my theory of transience, wax on about how we're all going to die.

Nah, not today. The time will come, but it's not meant for today. I decide to change the subject.

"Hey, Dad, what are you doing there?" I crane my neck forward and down to see what's in front of him.

"Just sketching something…" he says quietly.

Dad tries to cover up the yellow legal pad in front of him, like a defiant teenage boy stealthily sliding a magazine under his math book.

"Let me see. Come on, let me see, young man." I snap my fingers impatiently like my hyper vigilant high school geometry teacher, Brother Knapp, used to do.

I pull the pad out from under the newspaper.

"Hmm," I say, studying the top page. "Do you want to share with the class what you're doing there, young man?"

Pause, pause, pause. In linguistic transcription, we would code this as:

M1: Do you **want** to /**share** with the **class** /what you're **doing** there/ young **man**?

I study it, holding it up to the light and rotating it. It feels like a Da Vinci diagram, with wheels, axels, pulleys, levers, springs and gears that mesh with each other.

OK, Alex, I'll take Da Vinci inventions for 800 dollars... This sixteenth-century invention allowed for a person to propel forward...

"What is this, Dad? It looks like... a *ramp*?"

It had framing drawn in 3-D, angles marked, lengths and heights indicated. Everything precisely calculated. Notes on the side, in crisp engineer lettering: four point eight degree angle, twelve point five percent grade.

"Wow," I say. "It's a very detailed design. I think there is an engineering streak in your Dietrich genes." Dad's mother, Margot Dietrich, left a number of detailed drawings and sketches when she passed away. My son Christopher must have inherited a trace of this architectural gift as well, drawing detailed inventions from an early age.

"Yeah. It's a ramp," Dad confirms quietly.

"A *wheelchair* ramp?" I ask. I'm enjoying my school marm role.

"Mmmmp-hmmm," he concedes reluctantly.

"So you really think that…*maybe* she's coming back?" I ask him, point blank.

There's a long silence. He realizes he's been trapped. Snookered.

"I just thought…there's no harm in *preparing* for it," he says.

I look at him, trying to make eye contact, but he's gazing downward.

"Right, right," I say. "Yep, there's no harm."

We pause a bit more, stuck in time. These 'stuck moments' are happening more frequently now, becoming a part of our interactive grammar.

I take another look at the drawing, admiring its detail. "Well, tell you what, I'm going to go take a shower. Then maybe we can head over to Ellingwood for a visit, okay?"

"Mmm, okay," he says, glad that I've let him off the hook. No more explanation needed.

I hand the pad back to him. He takes it, looks up at me, with puppy eyes, pleading let's-keep-this-a-secret.

"So you won't tell your…um, mother…or Kate…about…?"

"Don't worry, Dad. I don't think they'd understand. I won't mention it to them."

He sighs in relief.

"And hey, great job, Leonardo," I tell him. "Next, you can work on a new helicopter design." I know this is a cruel twist of the knife, but somehow I can't escape the compulsion to inflict this pathetic German sense of humor that runs through our family.

I head down the stairs, then stop and turn to him.

"You know, Dad, maybe that's your superpower," I offer.

"Superpower? What the hell are you talking about?" He's back in character.

"You know, inventing stuff, offering fixes, even if people don't understand what it's for. Like Leonardo da Vinci."

"Leonardo the what?"

"You know, the Italian inventor, Leonardo *da Vinci*. He invented all kinds of stuff, scuba diving gear, helicopters, self-propelled vehicles."

"Ah," he nods. I'm sure he's stored away all of this information somewhere, accessible when he encounters a crossword puzzle cue or a Jeopardy question.

"Yep, he was way ahead of his time. He invented lots of stuff that people didn't know they would need someday. Like a wheelchair ramp."

Dad winces a bit at the dig.

Psycholinguistic slow-time silence. Preparing the stage for what to say next.

"You know she's not coming back, don't you?" I say.

He's become quiet again. *Pratayahara*, silence of receptivity.

"You never know," he says. "Never can tell."

"Well, you may well be right," I offer. "No harm in preparing."

He smiles softly, knowing I'll keep his invention secret, that I won't be rushing out to the copyright office to file a patent. He sheepishly stands up, grunts a bit, and sidles over to his enormous worktable in the living room.

He removes the green plastic tarp he has draped over it, in a single practiced sweep, laying the plastic sheet over the chair next to the table. Then he carefully places the wheelchair sketch in one of his manila folders and slides it gently under a pile of papers near the edge of the table.

13. *The Field Trip*

Families provide you a complex mix of baggage to carry with you through your life. I think of it as arriving at an airport baggage claim: you check the monitor for which carousel is handling luggage from your incoming flight, you jostle with the other arriving passengers to identify your bags. You're not sure which are yours or even how many you've got since you didn't pack them yourself. Dutifully, you take the bags off the belt, all that have your emblem on them. Some are attractive Rimowa spinner suitcases, others are tattered hobo bindles. But it's all yours, you got to claim it all. Got everything? *You're welcome.*

I know there's a science to this. It's not only genetic coding. It also includes — at no extra cost! — a collective belief system, kind of kludged together in response to a long history of family dynamics. I have no idea how long it took for the baggage to be packed, but everything going back probably five or six generations seems somehow connected to the present. I know that when someone dies and people are still around who remember them, they're not really 'dead' — they're still alive in the memories of those who knew them. In some cultures, they differentiate 'types of dead,' for instance, between the 'sasha,' the recently departed and the 'zamani,' those recalled by name only. But in my family, the 'zamani' goes back at least to the time that the original Bron, Dietrich, Hofmann and Meiser men made their way from various parts of Germany to Cincinnati.

My four great-grandfathers — Josef Dietrich, Tobias Bron, Walter Hofmann, and Maximilian Meiser — all made their way as young men, teenagers really, across the Atlantic to Ellis Island. Cultural refugees, and Lord knows what baggage they brought with them!

I'd like to think that I've unpacked — in some way deconstructed or examined or maybe simply observed — a good portion of the contents, but there are always little arcane gewgaws that I discover along the way. And that's *only* the male half of the equation.

One of the more endearing curiosities inherited from this morass of family lessons is encoded in the concept of 'aufsaugen,' as my grandfather Jake, my Dad's dad, called it. My best interpretation of this is the desire to observe something humbly, to listen closely without pre-judging, to absorb. He used to say that "you don't grow up until you realize that you don't know as much as you think you know."

You want to know why...?

My grandfather Jake didn't know much about formal science as far as I can tell, but he sure as hell knew a lot about how things worked. When I was twelve years old, he'd pick me up in his pink Oldsmobile Cutlass on the first Saturday of every month at precisely 8:35 a.m. for my orthodontist appointment. I had to be ready. He'd honk once and only once. (If he had to come to knock on the door, there'd be hell to pay.) Grandpa would drive me to the dental appointment in downtown Cincinnati, in the Fifth Third Center Building across from Fountain Square, the veritable heart of the city. My father said he didn't need to, but Grandpa insisted that he wanted to do it, even though it ate up his entire Saturday. "Good for me to show the boy a few things." *In loco parentis.*

As soon as I plopped into the passenger seat and buckled up, *cla-clink*, I knew I was in for an unpredictably wild ride. Every trip with Grandpa involved at least one of his "You want to know why…?" lessons. Some of them were about things he learned as a soldier in World War I. As far as I could gather, most of these lessons were about courage, about facing uncertainty and imminent peril, or about resisting the inclination to become complacent and give up. 'Give up' was kind of a trigger word for Grandpa. "Want to know why some people *give up*?"

He got particularly passionate about this lesson. He used to talk about "The Battle of the Barn" (I later learned he had said "Marne") and what I understood as "The Battle of the N" (I later learned it was spelled Aisne, the name of a river in France.) "Want to know what it's like to feel hopeless?"

One time though, the lesson was much closer to home. This time it was, "You want to know why some people are lazy?" At first, I thought he was talking about me, and I wondered how he could have divined that I had cheated on my arithmetic homework that week.

Then I realized he saw me staring out the window, gaping at a large group of men loitering outside a row of buildings. We had been driving down the Vine Street hill and had just crossed Central Parkway underpass. Suddenly, as we entered into the light side of the tunnel, the sidewalks were jammed with clusters of black men in white T-shirts and loose-fitting jeans. Many were loitering in slow motion on the sidewalks, some were sitting on the stoops of their apartments, virtually motionless, a few with brown paper bags perched next to them on the concrete steps.

I snap out of my trance. "I don't know, Grandpa," I offer. *"Die Faulheit? Die Trägheit?"* I answer, not sure of what these German words he taught me actually mean, but I know they're words that criticize. A thousand shades of criticism in German, I had learned.

Then it struck me. "Is it because they drink too much?" I was trying to recycle the key points of prior lessons, to show Grandpa that I really was a good student. He had previously pointed out to me that homeless people often had small bottles of whiskey in little brown bags that they kept in their pockets. "Comfort bottles," he called them.

"Why do they need bags to cover them up?" I had asked. It didn't seem practical to drink out of a bottle inside a paper bag. "Are they hiding it from somebody?"

"Yeah, they're hiding the truth from themselves, *kyah-kyah-kyah,*" he had answered, chuckling in his enigmatic way. "But the truth always reveals itself, *kyah-kyah-kyah.* Sooner or later."

But no, drinking wasn't the correct answer this time.

Grandpa shakes his head, as the light changes. "It's history. History gave them a bad break. *Bedauerlich*!" A new word for me, mental note of the context. I was discovering that there were countless words in German to express bad luck.

History? Bad break? I shrug. I have no idea what he's talking about, but it seems like he's ready to pounce on a deep lesson, a serious link to events in the past. I tug at my seatbelt — no, no escape possible.

"You know, the Civil War and all of that, was supposed to give them equal rights, but with segregation, they're still second-class citizens," Grandpa announces.

The Civil War?! Really, Grandpa? I'm just going to get my braces tightened, isn't that torture enough? I shrug that kind of 'I guess so' shrug that kids give when a lesson goes right over their head.

"You may not know this, but my grandfather Tobias came here in 1859, just a fifteen-year-old kid. A few years later, he's drafted into the army, fighting for the Yanks, trying to give these people their civil rights."

These people? Grandpa takes note of my confusion and adjusts the focus of his lesson. "Anyway, even when you get bad breaks, you got to move beyond your personal history."

Personal history? I survey the men sitting on the worn-down concrete porch stoops as we're stopped at a red light along Vine Street. They look so weary and it's only nine in the morning. It all feels sad and distant to me.

Recalling this conversation many years later as I drive down Vine Street with my father, I see Grandpa as Don Juan and myself as Carlos Castañeda, diligent pupil, sitting in the shade of a rock in the Sonoran Desert, writing frantically in my notebook. Say that again, say that again. I want to get it down verbatim this time.

Grandpa then launches into a mini lecture. "It's history and evolution, boy." I recoil every time he calls me "boy." "If you're not willing to move beyond your personal history, if you don't try… you know what I'm talking about?"

I nod. I get the drift of the urgency of his lesson, if not the details. "If you don't try to improve yourself, you'll become lazy. Then you think you're not in control anymore, and then all hell breaks loose."

He pauses while I take this in. The light turns green and the pink Olds rumbles onwards. *Vrrr-vrrrrmmmm.*

"You understand that, boy?" Grandpa asks. I figured that he called me "boy" when he was trying to make a serious point. I nodded apprehensively, signalling *good-enough-for-now* comprehension. 'Feigning comprehension' was a very important listening strategy for a boy growing up in my family.

Now visiting my father decades later, I see striking similarities between Dad and Grandpa Jake. Both very observant, both very judgmental, both full of theories about *everything*. Both keen to impart lessons to their offspring. But always in their own way, in their own time.

It's my second visit to see Dad since Mom moved to Ellingwood. I'm at the breakfast table with him, finishing my second cup of coffee. Watching as Dad rises from the breakfast table on this particular morning, I see a small opening to shake things up.

I suggest, "How about going on a field trip today?"

He pauses in mid-stride and turns toward me. "A what?"

"A field trip," I repeat slowly. "You know, go out there," I say, pointing theatrically out the front door, "and learn something new."

I see him struggling to get his mind around this veiled taunt.

"A little self-improvement couldn't hurt, you know," I say, in my best schoolmaster tone.

He's still processing this.

"Remember? We *talked* about taking some little field trips while I'm here," I remind him. The week before I arrived, I'd emailed Dad with suggestions about taking some little side trips together.

Dad is still pondering the gravity of this. I'm about to give up the battle for the day.

"How about the Greenview Café?" he blurts out.

My eyebrows spring upwards. My jaw drops. I would have given about one in a million odds of his suggesting this.

On several occasions in the past, I had tried to plant the same idea. I had been curious about the café, the place his father had opened back in the 1930s, when Dad was just a child. The place was still there today, under different ownership. Whenever I had mentioned the idea of visiting the café when my mother was around, Dad had always quickly dismissed the idea: "Maybe some other time."

I wasn't sure of the precise reason, but I gradually inferred that Dad was somewhat embarrassed that the neighborhood where he had grown up along Vine Street in Cincinnati had become 'kind of sketchy.' He probably didn't want to expose my mother to these seedier aspects of the city. Protection, one of Jake's Rules. And its corollary, don't even let the person you're protecting know that you're protecting them.

By contrast, the neighborhood where my mother grew up is still unscathed by urban decay, in a bubble almost. Actually, her old neighborhood was untouched by human history: it looked identical to the way it had when she was a child.

I can't believe my luck. "Perfect! Let's do it." This is either a severe memory lapse on Dad's part — he has literally forgotten that he has more or less declared the Greenview Café as 'off-limits' (some variation of the Protection Rule, which I haven't figured out), or it's something on his bucket list? Maybe, like me, he wants to, or needs to unpack some of his own baggage?

"Well, I still have to shave," Dad warns, squashing my enthusiasm a bit.

"We can go after you shave." I'm not going to be deterred.

Whatever his motivation is, I know it can be overridden by any of the several sins of memory. In particular, Sin #4 Suggestibility (incorporation of misinformation into memory due to leading questions, deception and other causes) could easily wipe away our plans, if I were to propose an alternate plan in the next ten minutes. Or more likely, Sin #5 Bias (retrospective distortions produced by current knowledge and beliefs) if he were to activate his current opinions about the Greenview Café, which I take are largely negative. Or, God help us, the ever-looming Sin #6 Persistence (unwanted recollections that people can't forget, such as the unrelenting, intrusive memories of post-traumatic stress disorder), if Dad were to recall what I gather are any number of intrusive memories relating to the Café, and his family situation when he lived there.

Please God, Please God, Please God, just let us do this, I keep repeating to myself.

Please let us get there.

Hopeful, I go off to shower and get dressed. I put on my green patterned Oh Baby! Hawaiian shirt and a pair of white chinos. I'm ready! As I search for my sandals in the living room, I hear the familiar *splish-splash* sound of Dad shaving.

I peek into his bathroom. "Are you almost ready, Dad?" I ask. He's whistling a tune while he's splashing around his razor blade in the sink. Sounds like *Here Comes The Sun,* by The Beatles.

"Ready for what?" he asks, as he stops whistling, pulling down the left side of his face to make it smooth for the blade.

Oh, my God! He's forgotten. "Ready to go?" I ask.

"Go where?"

"You know. We're going to the Greenview Café."

"But it's closed," Dad says. "It's been closed for thirty years."

Uh-oh. I'm going to have to dig deep into my bag of tricks to make this one work. "Yeah, it is closed now," I concede. "But they've turned it into a museum. The Jake Bron Memorial Museum, I've already got the tickets. Really hard to get. Come on, we can't miss this."

He exhales deeply and stands up from his stooped position over the sink. "Oh, I don't know. I'm still shaving," he moans.

"No excuses, Sergeant," I announce. "We're leaving at oh-nine-hundred."

It's already well past nine a.m., but I like the sound of the "oh-nine-hundred," and I know it will conjure up Dad's sense of military stick-to-itiveness.

"Yes, sir," he replies, pulling his chin in, and feigning a half-salute with the hand holding his razor.

That seems to have done the trick.

About a half an hour later, after fighting off still more suggestions to do this another day, we're in the car, my jet-black Hyundai Elantra, parked along the right edge of Dad's driveway.

I get Dad to put on his seatbelt, I press the automatic door locks — *cha-choot* — adjust my seat then check the mirrors.

I realize then that we're on our way to open some baggage. This is baggage I've been saddled with, the gnawing need I have to discover this… thing. This thing — a passion maybe? — that connects my grandfather and my father. And me.

I wonder: Do we somehow choose our families, our own karma, our own stories? Or just how to interpret them?

I glance over at Dad, wondering if he's cogitating on a similar train of thought. "Projection," they call this in discourse analysis. Projecting your intentions onto someone and assuming they are in harmony with them.

"Buckle up." We both pull our seatbelts across our chests and attach them, *cla-clunk*, in perfect harmony. "This is going to be fun," I promise him.

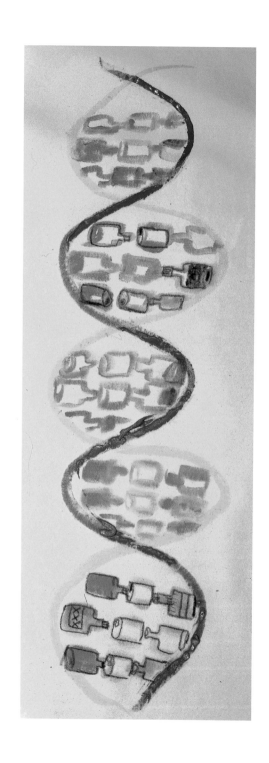

14. The GABA Gene

At Alcoholics Anonymous, they teach a kind of Buddhist philosophy, even though my guess is that the founders wouldn't have been able to distinguish a Buddhist from a Zoroastrian from a Unitarian.

What is taught in Buddhism is that the sensations produced by our engagement with life are illusory. Most people don't have a hard time grasping this lesson, or don't even think it's a lesson you need to learn. But for people who have this special GABA gene, we do have a hard time with this. That's the genetic piece of the puzzle.

If those same people have some trauma early in life, they're more likely to stumble into this trap. That's the experience piece. Then later in life, if we are sold on the promise that the pain of this trauma can be healed through the intake of some substance, the trouble ensues. That's the decision piece.

Those people, we the people, drink essentially because we initially like the effect produced by alcohol. First of all, we love the acknowledgement that there has been pain or confusion or unsolved conflict in our life. That's important, because we've been taught, seemingly, that whatever pain or struggle we've experienced isn't all that big a deal. We love the relief of this acknowledgement, the permission that it's okay to admit the truth. It's like the alcohol is talking to you, like you have a real relationship with it.

But the AA-Buddhism sect also teaches that the sensation of relief is elusive. Not just temporary, we all get that, but downright shifty, deceptive, slippery, and ultimately unable to be tamed.

Though we feel good while drinking — even amazing and spectacular — for a short time and though we feel, under the influence, that we can "fix" our problems — we soon become restless, irritable, and discontented when this feeling subsides, and the problems we thought we were fixing reappear.

But we keep coming back, ever hopeful of the possibility of self-discovery and self-renewal!

The best medical description that I've heard is that it's actually a "neurotransmitter" disease, perpetually giving a false reading.

But the Buddhist description is more compelling: You succumb to feeding the 'hungry ghost' of sensation again and again.

The genius of the AA founders was in hacking Buddhism, a centuries-old tradition of peaceful resolution of conflict. They convince the alcoholic that they can end the cycle of suffering, but not through prayer or meditation. The cure — or at least the key to permanent remission — is just to "follow a few simple rules."

The first rule is to admit that you've got a 'disease,' that you're predestined in a sense to obsess about fixing your life. It's an obsession, you're on the spectrum. Nothing you can do about the genetics. But there is something you can do about the past trauma, and there is something you can do about your decision with how to deal with it. You don't need to fix it, you just need to understand it.

And the magical fusion of East-meets-West in this is that the understanding, without the compulsion to act, is the fixing. Observe, breath, choose how to respond — or choose not to respond.

"What is that clown doing?" Dad fumes as we sit at a traffic light, rain streaking the windows. Somehow, Dad has this magical way of shaking me out of my reveries and daydreaming, a kind of a cross between a Marine drill sergeant and a Zen dharma teacher.

"Dad, it's okay," I say, readjusting to the reality of being stuck. "We have nothing better to do than wait in traffic."

"But you're *trapped* now," he says, pointing to the left lane of cars. "That guy's blocking your lane."

Yep, here we go again. 'Being trapped' is a major trigger for Dad. He can go ballistic if he ever feels ensnared by someone's devious intent.

"Dad, I'm not trapped. And just think, this extra time gives us an opportunity to talk. Waiting in traffic is a gift. Did you ever think of that?"

The pause and then the glare.

Dad doesn't like it when I do this, challenging 'the Rules.' You aren't supposed to flout the Rules: the tacit code of conduct Dad has been teaching me, pretty much incessantly, since I was a boy. The Rules, of course, are unspoken. Writing them down in black and white would violate the first rule, the rule of secrecy. Another one of the rules is now being invoked: do not show optimism in a difficult situation. Or maybe it was a convergence with another rule: Don't expect people to help you out. Make your way on your own. Sometimes it's hard to know which rule or rules are being summoned. These rules are anything but simple.

But either way, once I felt 'the glare,' I knew I was caught in a no-win conversation gambit.

I decide to change the subject. "Tell me something about the Greenview Café." I love having Dad as a captive audience. There's no way I could bring this up under normal circumstances. He'd wriggle out of it, jump up to grab a snack, or in his earlier days, pull out a cigarette.

Dad had always avoided talking about "The Café," a.k.a Jake's Café. I had always thought it strange that he referred to his father by his first name — I think this happened after Dad came back from the war. It was an expression of "I'm an adult now. We're on equal footing. You can't boss me around anymore."

"The café is closed, I keep telling you that," he says, with a note of finality, stropping a bit. This is the most brutal of the sins of memory: Persistence. Once you believe something, particularly if there's strong emotion attached, it's very hard to revise your belief.

I can see he's still unhappy about the traffic. And the idea that I tried to corner him with this interrogation.

"Yes, I know that," I tell him, lying, as I feel sure the Greenview Café is still in business. I haven't gone past it in years, but some things you just know. "Or at least it's not the same place. That's *why* we're going, remember? To find out what has become of the place. What it's like now."

I'm trying to convince him that it's in both our best interests to unpack this piece of baggage. *This is a* big *freakin' piece, Dad. We need to unpack it!*

I continue the probe: *"Why did your father open it to begin with? It was during Prohibition, right?"* I wait for Dad to acknowledge the context I'm conjuring up. He gives a barely perceptible nod.

"How did he expect to make money opening a bar during Prohibition?" I ask. Not what we call in linguistics a display question, something you toss out that you already know the answer to. I'm really wondering how money fit into the equation for his parents, Jake and Margot, raising four children. Money had to be a major concern. It still is with Dad, taking care of the money side of life is "a man's responsibility, pure and simple."

Dad leans back in the seat, adjusts his shoulder strap. Then he opens up with an insight he's never shared before. "Jake knew that Prohibition wouldn't last forever. Once it was over, the place would start booming."

Where did this bit of insight come from? Why didn't he mention this before? And how was he able to articulate such a complex idea?

I'm trying to get my head around this. First of all, I know that Grandpa Jake was no savvy entrepreneur. In his later years, he was always making cockamamie investments, generally losing everything. OK, got it! It must have been Grandma Margot who had figured this out. She always seemed to be the tempering force behind his decisions.

"Very prescient," I say. Dad gives me The Blank Stare. Wrong word choice. He of course knows words like *prescient* — and *oracular* and *vatic* and even *sibylline* — from years of intensive crossword puzzling, but he never uses any fancy vocabulary in conversation. It's unseemly, makes you stand out, draws attention to yourself. Another one of the Rules covers that: Who the hell do you think you are — calling attention to yourself?

Pulling up to the red light, I glance at the dashboard clock. It's 11:50 already. Uh-oh, I can almost hear the alarm sounding.

"What are we going to do for lunch?" Dad queries, right on cue.

"Well, Dad, remember. We're going to visit the Greenview Café and *then* we're going to have lunch," I say with an attempted air of authority. He doesn't seem to hear me. Dad is eying the tempting displays of Big Boys, Denny's, White Castles, and Skyline Chili joints along Reading Road.

It's going to be a hard sell, I think, but Dad gives in rather easily this time. "Oh, right," he says, vaguely recommitted to our plan. But I feel certain he'd abandon it in a second for the promise of a chili dog.

"It'll only be a short visit, Dad. Then we can eat wherever you want," I promise him.

I know that if we don't visit the café today, the opportunity will be gone forever. Then the Greenview Café will leave the 'zamani' — the part of personal history that is still alive in us — and become part of the 'sasha' — a part of untouchable history, known only by its former name — as soon as my father dies.

"Okay," he says. "Maybe they still serve sandwiches there," he adds.

One thing I remember from previous versions of the Greenview Café story is that the café used to serve soup and sandwiches. This was a kind of innovation for the time. Grandma Margot, who lived above the café with Grandpa and their children — Daniel, Renata, Lucy, and Madeleine — used to make the food and bring it down to the café.

In addition to her culinary prowess, Grandma Margot was the one who had the entrepreneurial gene. Her father, Jonas Dietrich, immigrated from Damme in Northern Germany to Cincinnati in the 1860s, at age fifteen. Just up and left, to jump on a ship from Hamburg and never turned back. Enough with inheriting the family business of potato farming and paying fifty percent in taxes to Kaiser Wilhelm. Jonas started his own grocery store in the Tusculum district of Cincinnati soon after arriving and did quite well for himself as a nineteenth century 'start up.' I used to swell with pride when I heard these stories. My ancestors were self-made men, not "sponges sucking up government money," as Grandpa Jake used to call anyone receiving public assistance.

According to Margot's plan, most of the income from the Greenview Café would eventually come from alcohol, but the soup and sandwiches were an added attraction to keep people coming in. Grandma was smart that way. She told me once that serving food kept people in longer, because they didn't get drunk so quickly.

Grandpa had mixed feelings about alcohol. Selling it was part of his livelihood, but he had come to understand its destructive power. He himself had stopped drinking shortly after he opened the café.

Why? I had always wondered. It seemed to me that one of the major perks of owning a bar is that you'd have free alcohol, all the time.

Grandpa had never answered me in much detail on a matter of such personal import — he was after all, the crystallizing force in 'Jake's Rules,' one of which was being very selective about who you confided in about your weaknesses. The only thing he said was that he came to know that he had "it, and once you know, you have to act quickly."

The "it" turns out to be the B-R3 version of the GABA gene, the "alcoholic gene," the one that binds aminobutyric acid in the neurotransmitters in the brain. The one that creates that beloved 'neurotransmitter disease.' Dad has it. I have it, too. If you get the BR-3 version, instead of the BR-1 or BR-2 version, jackpot!

You love alcohol and it loves you right back. A life-long symbiotic relationship. It's virtually guaranteed that you'll become addicted, if you just give it a chance. All you have to do is 'welcome the pirates aboard the ship.' *We mean no harm, promise!*

All you need to do is produce the conditions for the gene to thrive, particularly if you have any trauma in your past, just stimulate it. (And who doesn't have some trauma in their past?) Alcohol does the rest. Creates an insatiable yearning in the plasma membrane for a continuing rush of dopamine. They call this a craving. Oh, you still have to choose to satisfy the craving, start the 'illusion cycle,' but once you do, bingo! Off to the races.

I'm not sure exactly when Grandpa gave up drinking, but on one of my car trips with him, when we had spotted some homeless people drinking discreetly out of bottles inside paper bags, he told me that he hadn't touched "the varnish," as he called it, since shortly after Prohibition ended. "I've seen what it can do to people. It ain't pretty," he used to say. He often said "It ain't pretty" as a reminder to himself, I believe, not to go off on a verbal rampage.

"Get in the left lane. Turn left here," Dad orders as we approach Ross Avenue. He leans forward in his seat, jerking the seatbelt into his chest with an "ommph," surveying the historic landscape.

A piercing twinkle of recognition registers in his blue eyes. He's looking up at the discord of electric wires and bus cables as if studying a work of art. He's making sense of it all.

"Turn left here," he says again.

I knew that we were turning left a few streets too soon, but I certainly didn't want to overrule him, to break his reverie. I realize we could have arrived much sooner with a map app on my phone, but I wouldn't dare use a GPS with Dad aboard. Dad is the quintessential "I know the way," King of the Jungle kind of guy. To use technology to one-up him would be the most emasculating insult imaginable.

We circle the area of the café several times and finally home in on the location. He sees some kind of landmark, though it all looks like faded brown brick buildings to me. "There, there it is," he says, with a lift in his voice, like a sailor sighting land after months at sea.

I pull into the parking lot outside the café, crunching my Michelins over broken chunks of asphalt. I park between two abandoned vehicles, a creamy white Cadillac with a broken passenger side window, covered with blue duct tape, and a faded brown Chevy Citation hatchback, with a crumpled hood and two flat tires in the back.

Now we really *are* trapped. There's no turning back now. *Om maṇi padme hūṃ*, the Buddhist mantra for spiritual efficacy is calling us to move forward with our mission. Our mission is to cross this threshold of persistent memory, to open the baggage and take a dispassionate look at what's inside.

I think we're ready. As they say in the AA-Buddhist circles, the hardest part is just showing up.

15. *The Inheritance*

We pause at the entryway of the café, standing stoically, timelessly on the corner, not more than six feet from the street. This will be one of those moments that flashes into your consciousness right before your death. It's not so much that what you discovered was so historic or earth-shattering, but that it was fateful — full of your own fate. That you decided to look inside.

I gaze across Greenview Avenue at the vastness of Saint Mary's Cemetery, where my Grandfather Jake and Grandmother Margot, Dad's parents, are buried. I start to say something about the serenity of the cemetery, but as I turn toward him, I notice that Dad is staring upwards. He's looking wistfully at the battered sign above the entrance to the café in front of us. And beyond that, to the second story, above the café, the weather-beaten brownish façade of the apartment where he grew up.

He exhales deeply and looks back down at me. We make eye contact. *Do we really want to go through with this?*

I marvel at the fact that we've come this far. I nod an overconfident "let's do this" gesture. Bonnie and Clyde, Butch Cassidy and the Sundance Kid, Frank and Jesse James. Weary Willie and Meek Mike. We're ready for the shootout at the O.K. Corral. Or so I think.

Be careful what you wish for.

I push gently on the door. It creaks open. The place is dark and cool, a remarkable contrast to the searing heat and blazing light of the day outside. There's a pungent odor of smoke and dust. We step inside warily. I go first, holding the door open for him to follow me.

Our eyes adjust. The place is sprawling, covering a vast open area. Easily twenty square wooden tables, evenly placed around the room, each with four chairs tucked around it. A thin commercial Holytex carpet, once lime green, I imagine, but now a pukey avocado color, stretches from wall to wall, with ripples throughout. Light from the TV above the bar reveals an intricate mosaic of mocha colored stains on the carpet. A large squarish C-shaped bar is in the center. It has a worn-down, tan Formica top.

We scan for signs of life. No one is inside. *Oh, wait, over in the corner*, look. A balding man is hunched over an arcade game. Vague alien-like *vvvv-vvvv-vvvv* synthesizer sounds waft into the room. I drift closer, leaning backward like someone navigating a trail along a cliff, and notice a cigarette burning in an ashtray on the left side of the control panel, and then a partially full whiskey glass on the right side. I try to make loud shuffling noises, wondering if the player is going to turn to look at me. Finally, he does a quarter turn in my direction, his body still facing the console.

"Does anybody work here?" I ask, in a louder voice than usual, trying to project across the room.

"*I* do," he says, barely moving a muscle. Poker face.

"Oh," I say, a bit disappointed that my chummy opening gambit didn't draw a more cheerful response

Now what?

I think about pouring out our story in a kind of stereotyped Gabriel Iglesias standup comedian voice: *Well, you won't beli-ee-eeve why we're here. My father and I — that's him over there, 'Hi-i-i Dad!' — were thinking, you know what we ought to do today — I know this is cra-a-azy but — we ought to go visit the café that your father owned back when you were a kid. Won't that be, like, just soooo much fun!*

Then I have second thoughts. Better not risk any problematic behavior.

"Could we have a couple of drinks?" I ask in an earnest customer-like voice.

He gives me a dubious stare. Maybe he's just really slow in responding, running everything through some kind of filter.

In most situations, the tension would have gotten the better of me, and I would have just said, "Never mind." But then I remind myself, what the hell? We have the right to walk into a public establishment and request service. Right?

What's the worst thing he can do: Shoot us?

Actually, yes, that's a real possibility.

The guy drifts back toward the bar, staggering just a bit. I nod to Dad to take a seat at the bar, at the corner nearest the door. We might need a quick getaway. Dad is following my lead, but I can sense he's already seen what he came to see. He's ready to leave. Mission accomplished. He seems perched for a quick exit.

Here's where Dad and I differ. In a new situation, I tend to take in as much as I can, which is often more than I can handle, and then try to process it all later. Dad has a much lower threshold of tolerance for 'horseshit' in any situation, familiar or unfamiliar. As soon as he detects *any* kind of disrespect, insolence, or effrontery, he launches into attack mode. I actually find myself using two hands, indicating calm down, or "keep it low in the strike zone," depending on your sport.

Dad slides onto one of the bar stools and I sit on the one next to him. The guy reluctantly moves around behind the bar and surveys his collection of liquor bottles, as he moves toward the elbow of the bar in front of me.

"Actually, we'd like two Diet Cokes," I say, trying to talk above the din of the television. He looks at me like I'm crazy.

I assume in the few steps to get from the game console to the bar, he came to terms with the fact that two alcoholics have managed to find the only bar in the neighborhood that was open before noon and were raring to start tanking up for the day.

"Co...?" the guy repeats in a sparing barroom mumble. The parsimony principle of communication. Say only the minimum needed for comprehension.

I nod. Close enough. I'm willing at this point to drink whatever he decides to serve us. If he poured me a shot of Jack Daniels, I'd probably knock it back, just to prove I don't need a mediator to communicate with the locals. Or maybe just to get along. *This is why people drink*, I think to myself. Just caught up in a muddle of tangled relationships and scrambled expectations and misinterpreted signals. *Why go against the grain?*

My eyes have finally acclimated to the cave-like setting. I can now see the guy more clearly in the light of the TV above the bar. He's probably in his sixties, with splotchy ashen skin under a two-day gray stubble. He has a somber expression on his face, cheeks drooping, too tired to offer any playful repartee to his new guests. His shoulders are slumped forward. In spite of his coarse appearance, there's a handsome tough-guy quality to the guy, a bit of a Charles Bronson look. But now he's clearly worn down. Lost his zip, his charisma. Defeated.

I know, why don't I cheer you up: I'll put a quarter in the juke box and play an upbeat delirious spiritual song. Maybe Toby Mac's #1 Christian single: Made to Love. La-la-la... And daddy I'm on my way, I was made to love you, I was made to find you, I was made just for you... *You just need a little guidance. This is your lucky day! A visit from Jake's Witnesses. We're here to teach you about love.*

Dad is not as amused as I am. He stares at the guy in silence. I can tell he's ticked off. Something the guy has done — or more accurately, something he hasn't done — has really got him fuming.

The sound of the TV soap opera is blaring. I think it's *The Young and the Restless.* "I *know* it's none of my business..."

"You're right, it *is* none of your business..." Even for Dad, it's too loud. It's also too loud for me to ask Dad what he's thinking, so I try to read his body language.

Ah hah! Lips pursed, forehead a deep shade of red. Some code violation has occurred here. He's waiting for a sign of acknowledgement from the bartender guy. *Don't you know who I am?* There's not even a glimmer of recognition.

The guy fumbles around in some sliding doors beneath the bar and plops two cans of Diet Coke in front of us, with two soft clear plastic cups, half full of ice. Nice touch. I didn't even see him dip into the ice chest. I'm impressed with his smooth moves.

He says something. Sounds like "Suh..." Six? Seven? How many syllables? I wonder. I don't want to ask him to repeat. I fish into my wallet. I pull out a twenty-dollar bill, hoping this will cover it.

The guy scoops up the bill, turns to the cash register in a single sweep. Minimal movement to complete task. Skills galore.

I turn to Dad. He's still seething. I want to say, "Hey, Dad, isn't this fun? Aren't you glad we came on this field trip?"

Instead, I turn to him, lift my plastic glass and propose a toast: "*Zum wohl!* To field trips. To self-improvement. To Jake."

"Whatever," Dad mutters under his breath, gives a mock toasting gesture and takes a swig of his drink.

"I'll be back," I say. "Just going off to the men's room." I can see it's back by the gaming area, so I stumble past the video machines — *Call of Duty, Gears of War, Fight Night*, all pretty violent stuff — and enter the darkened men's room. Inside are two crumbling brownish porcelain urinals, a couple of brown dented metal stalls, and a washbasin tilted at a thirty-degree angle from the wall. As I pee and zip up, I take a lingering look at my surroundings. This may be the most neglected restroom I've ever been in, and I've seen my share of third-world loos. Not outright filth — no excrement on the walls, no urine pooled on the floor. Just the utter disrepair, the hopeless sense of abandonment. Caked layers of rust around all the exposed pipes, discolored sink and toilet bowls, the detached hinges from the stall doors, the cracked tiles of the floor, broken glass in the window above the urinals. Nothing has been attended to.

As I return to my place at the bar, I look at Dad, wondering if he's been able to break the ice with our host. I can sense that the guy is simply not willing to engage with a graying old man who just ordered a soft drink.

Turning on my bar stool, I decide to change tactics. I clear my throat. The bartender looks at me through half-opened eyes. "His father, Jake Bron, used to own this place," I say to him, nodding toward my father, hoping to rekindle the conversation.

Then I think it might be interesting to engage him in a little barter. Maybe start out with: *We want to buy it back, it's a family heirloom. Name your price.*

The guy reaches down to the ashtray under the counter and takes a drag from his cigarette, pondering. A long ash falls on the bar in front of him. Aposiopesis. Pregnant silence.

Twenty seconds go by. He finally exhales. "Must have been a long time ago," he says with just a touch of curiosity.

"Yeah," I say, now feeling chipper. We're really connected now, strangers sitting in a bar having a friendly chat. A *kumbaya* moment. See, I can do this!

"He sold it in 1959," I add, probing for more curiosity from the bartender.

Dad quickly jumps in. "Yeah, around that time." These dates all seem very recent to me.

The bartender takes a drag from *another* lit cigarette, this one in a black plastic ashtray at the end of the bar. I look over my left shoulder at the arcade machine, where a third cigarette is still burning in an identical black plastic ashtray. Multi-tasking. Actually, it's the second sin of memory, absent-mindedness, a particular scourge for alkies. It's not that they're forgetful, not that they have trouble remembering what they've done, it's that at the time they decide to do something, they don't actually intend to remember.

Dad has his own agenda, so he doesn't notice the state of the bartender. He actually seems excited now. He continues, "My father opened the place during the Depression, called it the Greenview Café because it's at the corner of Ross and Greenview." Caesura. Theatrical touch.

Water over the bridge. No response.

Dad is sure that the noise from the television is interfering with the flow of the conversation. "I wish he'd turn down the damn TV," Dad says to me, aggravated now at the absence of interaction. "Can't hear a damn thing I'm saying."

I contemplate for a moment jumping over the bar and switching it off myself. Then I envision the police interview: *Two young punks walk into a bar, trying to rob me. Officer, it was self-defense. I* had to *shoot them. They jumped over the bar. I didn't know what they were going to do next.*

Dad plows ahead in spite of the lack of uptake. "We moved here when I was in fifth grade," Dad says. I know this next part. "We lived upstairs, above the bar."

Here's an opening. "Who lives above the bar *now*?" I shout to the guy.

"I do," he says.

"Really, are you the owner?" I query.

"Nope. A guy named Kimmel is the owner."

"So how long have you worked here?" I ask.

"Twenty-nine years," he says, automatically.

"Wow," I say, looking around again at the decaying surroundings, wondering how someone would let the place deteriorate like this. "That's a long fucking time." I don't know why I decided to add a swear word, just seemed like a guy thing to do.

"Yup, twenty-nine years," he says again. "Long time." Ellipsis. Parsimony. Using just the minimum number of words to convey his idea. Pure poetry.

At first, I wonder if he's telling the truth. Then I think, what the hell, it doesn't matter whether he's telling the factual truth or not. At least he's talking about the café, the historic truth we came to connect with.

I look at the guy more carefully this time. Is there a story in this guy's face? What would motivate someone to work here for that long? Maybe he likes the perks? Penthouse apartment? Unlimited booze? Stimulating patrons?

"I'm going to the john," Dad announces.

Damn! I think. *No, you don't want to see that.* I'm wondering if there's a way I can discourage him.

But Dad has already made a beeline for the back corner. I guess he knows where the bathroom is.

"How's business?" I ask the guy, now that Dad has disappeared.

"Terrible," he confides.

In linguistics, we call these responses, virtually everything the bar guy is saying, "dis-preferred responses" — saying exactly the *opposite* of what the speaker expects to hear, the exact response that will kill the flow of the conversation. This guy is a master of response design.

"Just getting by?" I ask, undeterred.

"Yep," he says.

The guy lights up another Marlboro for ashtray number two as Dad returns. Now I see his talent as a kind of circus juggler, keeping multiple cigarettes burning. Light rhythmic coughing. I watch the guy's body bounce in cadence with his coughing.

"I don't get it," Dad fumes, now returned from the restroom. He doesn't sit down. He grabs his dark blue Notre Dame cap from the stool, obviously ready to leave.

"Want to finish that?" I ask him, gesturing my nose towards his half-finished Diet Coke.

"Nope," Dad says, turning toward the door decisively. Dad has now joined the monosyllabic conversation club.

I pick up the three one-dollar bills from the counter. I leave the ten-dollar bill on the table.

Dad doesn't miss asymmetrical transactions like this. "That's ten dollars! Are you crazy?"

"It's for the stimulating conversation," I say. Dad tries to muster a smile.

I make a big to-do about pushing the stools back to the bar, hoping the guy might implore us to stay. He doesn't. Or maybe invite us upstairs to see Dad's childhood apartment, which would have been more emotional input than we may have been able to absorb. No luck on that front either.

As we turn to leave, I ask, "What's your name?"

He does a quarter turn and coughs out a kind of monosyllabic bark. *Horch Kwuml.* Something uninterpretable. Clears some phlegm at the same time. Multi-tasking.

"What did he say?" Dad mumbles as we ling stumble out the doorway, down the two concrete steps, into the sunlight. It's still empty out here. Still too early for the alcoholics and drug addicts to emerge into the daylight.

"He said, 'thanks for coming. Hope to see you again soon.'"

"Fat fucking chance," Dad snarls, pulling on his baseball cap.

"Yes, exactly," I repeat to him. "Fat fucking chance."

I can see he's rattled. "Well, that was something," I say. "Thanks for taking me here today."

Yeah, sure, he nods.

I reach for my key in my pocket and we head out, across the gravel parking lot, in the oppressive heat, toward the car. I notice that Dad is holding onto my arm.

This is new— he's never leaned on me before.

16. The Protection Code

I have learned from my occasional forays into Buddhism that there is a pause between your in-breath and your out-breath. If you can learn to lengthen this pause, if only by a millisecond, you can find a 'space' to construct meaning out of something you have just witnessed, an instant of time to let in a missing piece of memory that will clarify your understanding. Damn, I need a big pause now, some space to figure out what has transpired inside the Greenview Café. We walk back to the car, more like shuffling, in the intense July heat.

The heat perhaps triggers the recall of the rest of my Snake Dream from that morning:

I've arrived in Miami on a steamy morning for a special mission, to confront the snakes that wish to kill me. My guide, a tall thin white man, greets me at the airport. He shakes my hand heartily. He's dressed elegantly all in white, his silver hair slicked back under a Panama Hat. His driver, a well-built black man, in a shiny gray suit with an open-top purple shirt, waits for us outside in a pure white Rolls Royce Phantom.

The driver takes me to a hidden Mayan ruins — who knew there were Mayan ruins here?! — full of intricate stone carvings of gods. The area, once a majestic place of worship, I gather, is now deserted, overgrown with vines. Some vines are emerging from the eyes and mouths of the carved gods.

I descend from the car. I turn to look for my guide to ask what is next, but he has disappeared.

I decide to proceed toward the middle of the ruins, hacking my way forward through the vines with my hands. Marching silently toward the center of the ruins, I come to a square opening. I hear a hissing sound and notice a colorful striped snake curled on the ground.

I look the snake in the eyes. "It's you," I say. I'm not afraid, but I know this is the one that has been evolved to kill me.

The snake looks at me respectfully, even with a sense of compassion, and lets me know somehow through its narrow gleaming red eyes, that he will make this process as painless as possible. But it must be done, he says. The snake does not articulate this in my language, but I understand that this is not intended as a personal attack on me, that it must adhere to its own 'code of protection.'

Dad and I have now trudged back across the lot where my rental car is parked, between an aging Cadillac and an old beat-up Chevy hatchback. Time feels distorted. This walk may have taken us ten minutes, I don't know. Parataxic distortion. To my surprise, the car is still there. No windows broken. I pull out my key fob and bee-beep the doors open. I help Dad into the passenger seat. He closes the door feebly. I reopen it, help him with his seatbelt, and slam the door shut. I get in the driver's side.

We sit quietly for a bit, both breathing deeply, absorbing the moment. Inhale, pause, exhale. What the hell just happened?

"Well, that was a life-changing experience," I say.

"That guy's a *Schwachkopf*," Dad pronounces.

Outside of my German vocabulary, but I kind of get the drift: The guy's an *asshole*.

I wait for a little more detail on his assessment. "Doesn't show any curiosity. Looked like he was half-dead," Dad says, shaking his head slightly.

I start the car, wait for the air conditioning to kick in.

"Let's go to Valentino's for lunch," I suggest. "You must be hungry." This is his favorite restaurant. It's in Reading, a safer part of the city where I grew up.

We ride for a few minutes in silence. I'm wondering why my worldly charm didn't work on Horace. Why he wouldn't open up to me, share his feelings. Dad seems to be stewing over something.

"I'm going to call some people," he announces, as we drive along Vine Street.

"Call who?" I wonder.

"I'm going to call some people," he says. He rattles off some names: "Gus Wertheimer, Herbert Zimmermann, Helmut Kruger."

"Who are they?" I ask, curious.

He's fuming. "I know some people from the city office. I'm going to ask them to look into what's going on down there. They can't get away with that," he says.

I'm thinking about the lesson here: Right. You're going to turn this whole thing around. One of Jake's Rules: You can fix *anything*.

I turn toward him. "You know, Dad. It's okay. We tried. Things change. Nothing needs to be fixed."

He's quiet for a while. Then he says softly, "I wish you didn't have to see that."

I smile at him, searching for his eyes, now cast downward. "Still trying to protect me, huh? Protect me from the cruel paradoxes of human fate."

"Yep, I guess so," Dad says.

We ride a bit further. I turn right from Vine Street onto Galbraith Road.

"You know, Dad," I offer, "maybe the guy's just burned out. It's not his fault. You know what I mean?"

Dad looks up at me, puzzled. *Why on earth would I sympathize with a guy like that?*

"He's probably heard so much meaningless drivel in his day that he just assumes that everything he hears is horseshit." When used judiciously, "horseshit" is the quintessential bonding term for Dad and me. Dad believes there is a massive conspiracy of "horseshit" in the world, and he appreciates when I empathize with his perception.

The explanation doesn't help though. He's not thinking about conspiracy theories now. "My father worked his butt off to make that place a success," Dad says, overriding me.

We're stopped for a light at the corner of Anthony Wayne Avenue, in front of the McCluskey Chevrolet Used Car Superstore. I put my elbows on the steering wheel and cup my eyes with my hands.

"I know that," I say. "I know that."

I look at him to be sure he understands. I wait for him to look back. He finally does, melting a bit. His chin is quivering and some drool is leaking out from his lower lip. I think I see some moistness in his eyes.

We ride in silence again. Dad stops giving me directions, stops caring if we get somewhere on time, stops attempting to help me avoid any more bad drivers on the road.

I miss the left turn onto Reading Road, but Dad doesn't spout his customary chidings about me not knowing the best route to get somewhere. We make our way to Valentino's by looping all the way around Ridge Road and Benson Street, past the neighborhood where my mother grew up. Dad doesn't seem to mind the detour, the delay.

He's barely moving at all.

I turn off of Reading Road onto Zeigler Street to go into Valentino's. I notice that the main lot behind the restaurant is full, so I pull into the lot across the street. I help Dad out of the car. He grabs my elbow this time. We trudge toward the back door of Valentino's.

Dad always wants to go into Valentino's through the back door — it's one of those family customs that had some original purpose which is long forgotten — so we weave in through the back parking lot. Slowly, very slowly. Step by step. The Matrix Effect. Everything has slowed down. The Specious Present. There is ample time to take in the surroundings: As we walk through the parking lot toward the back entrance to the restaurant, we are engulfed in wafts of toxic fumes coming from Carl's Auto Body Shop. A handful of workers are busy repairing wrecked vehicles, one guy with an air paint spray gun applying a fresh coat to the fender of a metallic blue Mustang, another with an air sander, another with a grinder, all contributing to a cacophony of car body repair theatrics. I notice that none of them are wearing masks. *Caution to the wind! Real men at work!*

I try to hurry Dad along to the restaurant door, but there's no way to pick up the pace. And he doesn't seem to mind the fumes. As we near the building, he tells me, perhaps for the hundredth time, "This place used to be a truck stop, you know."

"Oh?" I say, as if it's the first time I've heard this curious bit of local folklore.

I push in on the door. We step inside. It's suddenly cool, dark, familiar, and comforting. Voices surround us. Everyone seems to know everyone. Chatter and laughter. Smiling, signed portraits of celebrities born in Cincinnati adorn the walls of the entrance foyer: Stephen Spielberg, Roy Rogers, Doris Day, Neil Armstrong, Annie Oakley — wait a second, a *signed* photo of Annie Oakley? Was she actually here? William Howard Taft and Helen Taft, Sarah Jessica Parker. But no Charles Manson, I notice. He was also from Cincinnati. I guess they want to preserve their squeaky-clean image.

We are shown to a booth, an overly broad slab of white laminate, with deep, worn-down green plastic seat cushions. The waitress plops some oversized menus on the table. "Be right back," she chirps.

We slide in, plunge down, down, down into the soft seats. Dad exhales, a lengthy wheezing sound. The TV blares from over the bar. The wall opposite us, behind a piano, is covered with rows of faded paintings of clowns. Most resemble Weary Willie, the sad and tattered clown from the Ringling Brothers Circus. The clown who is left sweeping up the ring after the other performers. I start studying them. Do they have names too?

Dad has settled down a bit. The dark, the cool stream from the air conditioner, the familiar murmuring sounds all put him at ease.

"Dad?" I ask, pulling myself away from the hypnotic stares of the clowns. Bim-Bim, Snub, Kipper, Pee-Wee, Sprockets, Brony, Blinko. I've given them each a name.

"I'm curious," I continue. "What did Grandpa do when you came back from the War?"

He squints at me. This is a complete non-sequitur. *Where the hell did* that *come from?* With anyone else, he would continue his pattern of minimal responses, killing the conversation. But I just press on.

"Talking about the Greenview Café…" I say, trying to reset his memory. His look darkens a bit. I can tell he doesn't want to relive the egregious mistreatment we suffered recently at the hands of Horace, the bartender.

He's gone into a fog, disappeared from the conversation.

I try to forge on. "When you got married and moved away. When Grandpa realized you weren't going to come back and work in the café?"

No response. This will have to wait. Dad is perusing his menu. "What day is today?" He wants to know the daily specials.

"It's Wednesday."

He reads aloud from the menu. *"Oh, Wednesday! Bratwurst."* Dad enjoys this little bit of gamification on the menu. Spin the wheel, take your chances.

But wait, *bratwurst?* That's German. I thought this was an Italian restaurant. I've never been able to make heads or tails of Valentino's hybrid menu. I guess we should be thankful it's not kidney stew.

I repeat my question. "What did he do? What did Grandpa do when you told him you weren't going to take over the café?"

Dad glances up. "He eventually sold the place. He started a business as a paper carrier. He had a *Cincinnati Post* route. He was good at that."

That's good enough for me. End of interrogation. Karmic circle completed.

Dad is hungry. No more talking, I assume, until he gets something to eat. "But that was his dream," Dad offers. "He'd always wanted to do that. Have his own place."

I look down at the menu. I feel a memorial pang of indigestion. I close the menu quickly.

His dream? Dad said that? "I didn't know guys from Grandpa's generation had dreams," I retort.

Dad understands this is a wisecrack. He nods. "Sure they did."

"Well, he did it," I confirmed. "Went for his dream. Good for him."

"Yep, he did it," Dad repeats.

"Are y'all ready to order?" A pleasant voice cuts in and breaks up our little sashay into the past.

Dottie, her name plate says. Dad surveys her up and down. A bit too much leering, I think. She doesn't seem to mind. Part of the job.

"I'll have the brat special," Dad announces. "And I'll have a piece of coconut cream pie later. And some coffee. With cream." He pauses, waiting for her to get this all down. She doesn't write anything. "And some extra napkins," he adds, allowing just enough ambiguity about how many he wants and when he wants them so that he can pester her later.

"You got it, hon," Dottie says, cheerfully. She's probably handled the likes of Annie Oakley and Charles Manson. This old guy wearing a Notre Dame cap isn't going to get the best of her.

"And you, sir?" Dottie says.

I never quite feel like a "sir" when I'm with Dad, but I realize she is talking to me.

"Nothing to eat for me just now. Just a Diet Coke, please."

"You got it, hon," Dottie says with exactly the same intonation. She turns and walks toward the bar. Dad gives her a subtle wink of approval.

"Did I tell you?" Dad says. "This place used to be a truck stop. Truckers would stop here. Reading Road was a big thoroughfare. Connected Cincinnati and Dayton. The only real road. Wasn't called Valentino's back then, though. I can't remember the name. But all the truckers liked to stop here. A real peaceful place."

"Shelter from the storm?" I offer, citing a favorite Bob Dylan song.

He doesn't get the reference, but he nods.

In this moment, Dad is finally able to exhale. He is back in his element, the cool air of Valentino's, the comfortable decaying cushions of the booths allowing us to sink into the cozy familiarity, the contentment, the protection of being treated like kings.

17. *The Secret*

As your trusty narrator, I want to reframe the story a bit here. Most people tend to live their lives rationally. Most of us will accept some version of 'Pascal's wager': that we're spiritual beings having a human experience. Or even if we're not, if we're just these flesh-bound biocomputers living out a timed existence on Planet Earth, it's still a sound bet to behave *as if* we are boundless spiritual beings. Nothing to lose.

For either side of the wager, memory is the cognitive faculty that makes life meaningful. It's actually the part of us that allows us to create meaning, that lets us intertwine the fabric of our experiences. Memory allows us to reflect, to transcend present moments. Memory keeps track of who we are and where we are on our journey in the world.

As my sister Kate said, while she witnessed my mother's decline over the past couple of years, the worst part about her dementia is *not* the forgetting the names and places and activities and routines. That stuff is all trivial. It's that she has been losing her sense of *who* she is, what has made her who she is, even what she loves. As the disease progresses, she loses more and more, and the glimpses into her memory, who she really is, become increasingly rare.

As memory begins to fade and malfunction, as I am noting in both of my parents' decay, it feels urgent to try to 'save' what we can. When I lived in West Africa, I often heard the saying (I found the Togolese to be particularly adept at quoting axioms!), *Un vieillard qui meurt, c'est une bibliothèque qui brûle.* "When an elder passes away, it's as if a library has burned."

Everything stored in their memory has passed with them.

Memory can be revered, but it is not to be trusted. In psychology there's a theory about the 'seven sins of memory.' These are the natural tendencies of human memory to alter the recall of what actually happened in the past, generally to serve some higher purpose than just getting things right. I think of these 'sins' as clever guiles of mind that allow us to exercise our imaginations and see ourselves in new lights. I use a mnemonic device, The Seven Dwarfs, to remember these sins: Tranny (transience), Absinthe (absent-mindedness), Bollocks (blocking), See-Saw (suggestibility), Bossy (bias), Periwinkle (persistence), and Little Miss Muffet (misattribution). In a way, the sins all 'help' us to call back events in a safe way — differently from what objectively transpired to be sure, but in the end, in a way that is more serviceable, more kind to us. Who on earth wants to remember things as they actually happened?

If you add the effects of aging and disease and fatigue, my chances of communicating coherently about memories with Mom and Dad are becoming thinner and thinner by the minute. I can visualize the moment when everything has simply burned.

Dad and I are now in a state of post-greasy-lunch glow, so I decide to try to probe some memories out of Dad. My sense is that these little memory talks are a pain for him, but I think he enjoys the interplay and the chance to indulge in some of his past glory.

"Hey, Dad," I jump in. "Do you remember a guy who used to live in our old neighborhood, kind of a wacko guy? You had a run-in with him once?" This story, from about the time I was ten years old, is one of those loose ends in our relationship that I'd like to tie up.

Dad looks up from his piece of coconut cream pie. With this little bit of sugar rush, he's much more attentive. "You mean Ashwood?" he says. That's the only neighborhood in Ohio I personally knew — we moved there, new construction, when I was a toddler and lived there until Dad got transferred to Detroit when I was starting high school — but I realize he's lived in several different Cincinnati neighborhoods.

"Oh, I had a lot of run-ins with guys there." He shakes his head, and I'm not sure if he's ashamed or proud. One thing about Dad, he never shied away from a confrontation. His soldiering experience in World War II gave him a warrior's mindset: Be ready to die on any given day, in any given encounter. Dignity under fire.

"Really?" I ask. "I can only remember a couple of times you had arguments with the other dads in the neighborhood." What did Dad do during his off hours, go around picking fights?

"More than a few," he confesses. "There were a lot of clowns in that neighborhood. I really don't like to take horseshit from clowns, you know that." In his later years, after he retired, Dad started using the generic term "clown" to cover any variety of miscreant, malefactor, wrongdoer, or frankly, anyone he just didn't like. In his heyday, he would have used the word *asshole* over *clown* in this situation.

I know I'm pressing my luck, but I recount for him an event that took place when I was ten, on 'Devil's Night,' the night before Halloween. A couple of friends, Rusty, Dags and I were wandering around the neighborhood after dark, using pea shooters to shoot small navy beans at people's windows and then run away, laughing. It was pretty innocent fun for a pre-Halloween night. Occasionally, people would open their door and shout at us, but most people just ignored the little pranks that kids played.

One exception was Mr. Snyder. He was a burly guy, in his early forties, who always wore military fatigues and big black combat boots. We decided to target his house, secretly hoping to get a rise out of a man who was considered the neighborhood bully. We certainly did. As soon as the first barrage of peas hit his window, he was outside his door, pouncing off the porch like a cat, chasing us. Being the slowest of the three, I was grabbed from behind and slammed to the ground.

He jumped on my back and rubbed my face in his lawn, swearing at me, saying things like, "So you think you're a big shot running around scaring people, do you? Well, next time, I just might beat the shit out of you." It was terrorizing: all a blur of threatening words and choking sensations.

I was shaken and decided I didn't want to continue the Devil's Night pranks with my buddies. Humiliated, I stumbled home, hoping to sneak upstairs to my room unseen. No such luck. As soon as I walk in the side door of the house and step into the kitchen, Dad sees me. "What the hell happened to you?" he asks, seeing me tousled and teary-eyed.

I tried to explain in the most euphemistic terms I could assemble, but Dad was always able to see through my attempts at lying and put it together pretty quickly. "So you shot some peas with a peashooter at Snyder's window, and he came out and chased you, then beat you up? That's what happened?" I nod.

And then Dad said something like, "Well, that's not right. Let's go have a word with Mr. Snyder." *Now?* I'm thinking. *Do we have to do this now?* And he grabbed a jacket from a hook by the door, gave me a subtle eye gesture indicating I was to follow him, and off we went. I was scared out of my wits. Unlike my father, I had learned to *avoid* fights, and this seemed like the perfect formula for seeking out some serious conflict. There will be blood, I imagined.

The Snyder house was down the block on Clermont Drive. It took us a few minutes to arrive at his doorstep, and I was trembling all the way, hoping for a postponement. No such luck. We arrived in short order and Dad stepped up to the door. Two sharp knocks by Dad. *Bam-bam.* Mr. Snyder answered right away, as if he were a tiger jumping out of a bush, ready to pounce. As he stepped out onto his porch, he looked enormous to me, glaring down at us in his military fatigue pants and his big black army boots. I expected Dad to cower a bit, given this enormous physical presence. Instead, Dad stood his ground calmly and said something formal like, "Sorry to bother you, but we just came by to clarify what happened a little while ago." *Clarify?* I remember this was the first time I had heard this word.

Mr. Snyder sized up my father, a full six inches shorter than him, eyeballed me cringing behind him. Nothing to worry about here. Apparently liking his chances, Mr. Snyder launched into a taunt: "Well, *this* little asshole threw rocks at my window." I remember the shame at being called such a belittling name in front of my father, and realized Dad was now clearly triggered.

"I don't think they were rocks," Dad said, finally, still in his diplomat mode, ignoring the hyperbole. "But I'll have a word with him about respecting your property." Dad patted me on the back, indicating that maybe I should say something, but my heart was beating so fast I couldn't speak.

In retrospect, I think Mr. Snyder would have been wise to claim a victory at this point and accept this as an apology. But he insisted on escalating. "Well, you goddamned *better*," Mr. Snyder shouted. That phrase was a familiar affront in the Ohio Valley macho world, and even as a young boy I had heard it countless times. "He got off lucky this time, but if it happens again, I'll have to..."

Dad had reached his tipping point. He held up his hand and whispered, "You don't have to threaten us. I think we get the point."

With that, Mr. Snyder goads him with a loud "Oh, yeah?! Do you? Do you get the point?" and lunges forward. He reaches both his hands toward Dad's neck. I gasp. *My father's going to die!* And then in a flash I can only vaguely reconstruct, Dad twists and lowers his right arm across Mr. Snyder's outstretched arms, pulls him forward, and elbows him in the back of the head. *Swaaap!* Mr. Snyder crumples in a lump to the ground with a massive grunt. Game over.

I'm actually surprised at how vividly I can recall the scene, with the stream of angry invectives and flurry of quick actions, so many years later.

Back to the present.

Dad is leaning toward me across the table, trying to recall bits of the event, though it's obviously not so distinct for him. "Oh, yeah, OK, I remember." He mimes the hand and arm motions of the move that took Mr. Snyder down. "That's just a simple *krav maga* technique."

Krav maga? Where did he learn that? Ah, of course, in the army. There was a lot of stuff about his military life he never shared with me.

"I didn't really want to hurt the poor bastard, just teach him a lesson."

I let this sink in. "And protect me?" I proffer.

He pauses for a moment. "Well, yeah, protect you…" Intonation level, so he's going to continue. "But also protect me, protect the whole family. You know what I mean? You can't let a guy get away with threats like that."

I exhale and study his face. I don't remember it being all that rational. I just remember yelling, choking, grabbing, and punching.

"Yeah, well, you know what impressed me about that whole thing?" I ask. "Even more than the fighting techniques."

"What?" he asks, taking a sip of his coffee.

"Well, just your, um, resolve." I get that squint and the fertile silence again. "Your decision to act right away. Not like, well, I'll talk with him *next* time I see him. Or just letting the whole thing blow over."

Dad launches into a well-practiced mantra. "No, you got to take care of stuff like that right away. A problem like that isn't going to improve with age. Just going to get worse. And you're going to get worse too, living with it."

"Hmmm," I think aloud, "I guess you're right."

"Damn right I'm right."

Poetic.

"Well, you know, one other thing stuck with me from that day," I say.

Dad seems to be a bit embarrassed that we've been talking this long, kind of lingering on the edges of "war talk," but he lets me continue. He beckons to the waitress with his first two fingers circling his coffee cup, indicating he wants more coffee. This is probably the worst coffee in the world, as I recall from a previous visit — *why the hell would you want* more *of it?* — but maybe it goes well with their pie.

"What was that?" Dad asks.

I can see now that it's important to get through this story in little chunks and keep soft tossing questions to Dad. Otherwise, he'll just fade out.

I search for his eyes to get his attention back. "When we got back to the house, you know what you said to me?"

He shrugs. "I don't know" must be the most frequent phrase he's uttered throughout his lifetime sequence of conversations with me, but with a hundred different nuances.

I repeat the cue: "You know what you said to me after that incident with Mr. Snyder?"

A bit of Dad's wit bubbles up. He decides to play along. "Maybe I said, 'if you could have run faster, none of this would have happened.'"

I chuckle. "Maybe you said that. I don't remember. But you also said, 'Best not to tell your mother anything about this, okay?'"

Dad waits for the waitress, Dottie, to finish pouring his coffee before he responds. "Yeah, of course. You don't want to get her involved. Not your mother. *Oh, God, no.* Can you imagine? No, no, no, no, no. It's a guy thing."

"Wait, wait, wait. What does that *mean*? It's a *guy* thing?" I can tell he knows I've gone into journalistic mode, playing dumb, asking display questions, trying to get him to reveal stuff he'd rather not divulge.

"I don't know. It's just a… *guy* thing. That's what guys do, solve problems," he adds.

Solve problems! Hmm. What problem was solved that day? Lambasting a wayward neighbor? Putting on a krav maga exhibition? Rebuilding family harmony? Protecting your son from a bully?

"One of Jake's Rules?" I ask pensively.

Here comes that pregnant silence again. The Kappa Effect, perceptual time dilation. The waiting game. "One of Jake's Rules," he concurs finally, chuckling a bit in a way that actually sounds like Grandpa's *kyah-kyah-kyah*. "That's a good way to put it," he says.

"But what are Jake's Rules about? I've never really understood." I'm not in journalistic mode anymore. This is actually what I wanted to talk about. If I'm one of the chosen ones to inherit these rules, I'd like to know a little more of their etiology.

Priorities. Dad is now industriously scraping up the remnants of the graham cracker pie crust with the side of his fork. This screeching of metal on porcelain triggers one of those misophonic responses in me — but fortunately he's gotten every last crumb and the scraping stops.

"About? What do you mean about? Rules for … a … respectable life, I guess." He says, after searching a bit for the right word.

He raises the fork to his mouth, and sucks on it for a few seconds, staring up at the clown portraits on the wall.

"Anyway, that's how I remember them," he tells me, placing the fork down nimbly next to the pie plate.

Part Three: Connecting

Green Jell-O

Shoo-Flesh

My Bestfriend

Heartstrings

The Executive Report

The Bath

The Fall

18. Green Jell-O

There is a New Age concept, the Law of Attraction, which holds that we attract experiences and people to us based on our psychic vibration. Positive vibration attracts positive people and positive experiences. I'm sure this is true, but attracting the right people and experiences is not as easy as turning on a light switch: *OK, I'm ready. Let's go attract!*

At least it's not that easy for me. It takes me a little longer to plan what I want to attract.

I'm getting ready to visit Mom. I've taken longer than usual on my jog around Sharon Woods Lake, and then I stopped at Caribou Coffee for a morning latté and one of their crumbly scones. All this pushed back my intended visiting time by a good hour or so.

Verzögerung. Dillydallying, my Grandpa Jake would have said. He always had the right turn of phrase, and saying things in German — or often some mishmash of German and English — made the message sound so much more urgent. *Bring deinen Arsch in Gang! Get your ass in gear*! *Your odds ain't gonna improve by waiting.* He's probably right. But somehow I get the feeling that something strange is going to happen today. I might just be attracting the wrong things. Delaying the arrival of that doesn't seem like a bad idea at all.

It's already lunchtime by the time I arrive at Ellingwood — *how did I manage to waste this much time?!* I wander into the cafeteria and survey the scene. About sixty residents, all arranged in tables of three or four, at various stages of eating their lunch, with a staff of four or five aides roaming around trying to keep the peace.

I quietly pull up one of those white fan-back resin chairs that are everywhere in the cafeteria to sit beside Mom. She is sitting at her customary green circular table, with the number twenty-three perched on it, alongside her meal-mates, Fred and Sarah. Mom is staring straight ahead.

Fred gives me a nod of recognition, a kind of an elder-generation high-five and Sarah casts her mysterious glower over me — *Who are you and why are you here?* — but Mom doesn't notice me. She's now beckoning to one of the aides.

"Where's my milk?" Mom calls out.

"They'll bring it in a second, Mrs. Bron," one of the aides answers right away in a melodic voice.

One of the bussers passes by the table with his cart full of plates and glasses.

"Excuse me. Where's my milk?" Mom asks.

"We'll bring it out in a second, Mrs. Bron," he answers cheerfully.

One of the kitchen helpers, Edwin, is serving the next table. "Where's my lunch?" Mom asks, this time in a louder voice.

"We'll bring it out right away, Emma. You hold your horses," Edwin jokes with her.

Mom notices that her table mate, Fred, has already been served his lunch. She still hasn't acknowledged my presence. The justice of her lunch being served has taken precedence over all else.

"I'll have what he's having," Mom says to no one in particular, nodding her head in Fred's direction.

Fred is a charismatic man, large blue eyes, very tall, fit, seated regally in his wheelchair. Fred is always elegantly dressed, today in a chic green-checked Irish wool sweater. Though he seldom speaks, Fred always seems to have a calm awareness, a slight Buddha-like smile on his lips, as if he understands the 'dharma,' the secret meaning of life.

A slight tremor in his hands and head betrays his neurological condition. Fred's arm shakes, struggling to hold his spoon level, then dips down into his plate, and carefully brings the spoon up toward his mouth in a Ferris wheel type motion, quivering all the way. *Oh no.* He looks down, a bit forlorn. The contents of the spoon have spilled back down onto his plate. *Let's try this again.*

Every time I'm in the dining room, I now realize, the contents of Fred's plate is always green Jell-O. Nothing else. That's all Fred eats apparently.

I pat Mom on the arm, trying to encourage her to be patient. She acknowledges my presence for the first time, but then goes back to worrying: "Where's my lunch?" I imagine for a moment that it was Dad, not Mom, being denied his lunch. It would be: "Where the hell is my lunch? Do you people know who I am? I'm going to take these two here hostage until I get my freaking lunch!"

I snap out of my reverie. I turn to Fred. "How's your day been so far, Fred?" I have a chance at a 'normal conversation' with Fred, though I feel a bit like I'm betraying Mom from not at least *trying* to engage her.

"Oh, pretty good," Fred responds cheerfully. "I was at the Residents Committee meeting this morning. I'm on the board." He says "Residents Committee" with a certain air of pride.

A Residents Committee meeting? I didn't know that. I didn't know there was a Residents Committee. "What does the committee do?" I wonder aloud.

"Oh, we don't do very much," Fred chuckles. "We mostly just listen to people's complaints."

"Are there a lot of complaints?" I ask. It occurs to me that "complaints" is probably one of the top conversational topics among people of all ages, all walks of life, in all meetings.

"Oh, yeah. No end to the complaining," he concedes.

"Well, maybe that's enough, just listening," I say.

"Yep, all you can do sometimes," Fred says. I bet Fred has his own code, a sequence of phrasings and gambits that provide a glimpse to his inner workings. If I'm here long enough, he might share some of it with me. Look at me: The code breaker.

I wonder for a moment if Fred might ask me about *my* day. I would tell him about my jog around the lake in Sharon Woods, stopping by the Caribou Coffee, reading a story in the *New York Times* about… Then I realize: for the residents at Ellingwood, there is no Sharon Woods, there is no Caribou Coffee, there is no *New York Times*. This *is* the world. Right here. The dining hall at Ellingwood, the buffed white linoleum hallways with lanes for wheelchairs in either direction. This is all that matters.

Suddenly I feel 'the glare' from Mom. She has registered now that I'm talking with someone else. She doesn't like me shifting my attention away from her, chatting with Fred, or engaging in eye judo with Sarah.

Mom has just been served, finally! A sigh of satisfaction. She picks up the chicken leg from her plate, takes a deliberate, noisy bite, facing in my direction. *Crrrrrrunch.* Then she places the leg back down on her plate, starts to scrape away some of the deep-fried fatty coating on the outside, with loud friction-y motions. *Shhh-chhh-ssshhhh.* A sneer of disgust.

"I wasn't a picky eater until I came here," she informs me under her breath.

I think I know where this is going. Her voice begins to quiver. "And I can't cook anymore. I just can't remember how to cook anymore, she says. "I guess that's what's wrong with me. That's why they sent me here."

I guess this is a complaint. A grievance. A protest.

And it is true, I think. *That is why 'they' sent you here.* What are they — the five tests? Getting around by yourself, getting dressed by yourself, preparing your own meals, eating by yourself, going to the bathroom by yourself? Fail any of these, and they put you in assisted living. Fail all of them, and you're ready to sign a Do-Not-Resuscitate order.

"Well, they take good care of you here," I remind her.

"Oh, you're just saying that," she says, knowing that I'm humoring her. "They put me here because I can't remember. I just can't remember."

I pat her on the arm. She's right. When "you're old and in the way," they take you out, take you away.

Mom goes back to her chicken.

I decide to re-engage Fred, seeing if I can do this without offending Mom. I had learned in earlier conversations that Fred was from Akron, Ohio and worked for Goodyear Tire for forty years before retiring. He was also an avid golfer.

"What's your most memorable round of golf, Fred?" I ask.

It doesn't take him long to orient to the question and construct a reply. But he's still a little hampered in his articulation.

"F-F-F-F-Firestone Country Club, N-n-north Course. August 7th, a Sunday. I sh-sh-shot a seventy-two. H-h-hole in one on the fifteenth hole. Two hundred-twenty yards. Th-th-three wood."

Fred starts slowly and hesitantly, but once he gets on a roll, he's pretty fluent and fluid. "Magical," he adds, with a twinkle in his eyes.

Magical, I like that. *"Have you had a magical day recently?"*

Fred ponders for a moment. "O-O-O-Oh, not like *that* anymore. But…"

"But the magic is still inside, right?" I tap on my chest.

"Yeah, it's still there." He gives me the grin. Men communicate like this. Locker room repartee, teeming with vague niceties, replete with fist bumps and chest taps.

"No one can take that away," I continue, leafing through my repertoire of guy clichés for talking about emotions.

"Nope, no, they can't," he confirms. Fred goes back to coaxing a bit of green Jell-O in a circuitous route toward his mouth.

"I'll have what he's having," Mom says again, as an aide walks past.

"Maybe later, Emma," the aide, Loreen, says. She stoops down to look Mom in the eye. "But let's eat your meal first, okay, sweetie."

Mom temporarily drops her complaint, realizing that Loreen definitely *does* have her best interests at heart, and begins to scoop up some mashed potatoes from her plate. Her hand shakes a bit, but compared to Fred, her tremors are very mild, almost ballerina-like in their precision.

I turn to ask Fred about his work at Goodyear Tire. Pause. Wait for it. I'm actually enjoying the pause between the time that my question lands and Fred formulates an answer. "Th-th-th-that was a long time ago," he says. I'm thinking "that was a long time ago" is a universal expression of "let's not go there."

Mom's eyes open and tense, her jealousy rising again. She won't allow this switching of attention.

"I'll have what he's having," she says again, a bit louder, this time to me.

"No, Mom," I say firmly. "This is your meal. You get what you get."

Fred snickers. I think he's enjoying this little play on words. Fred has previously lectured me on the relative seriousness of the maladies of every tenant at Ellingwood: *We've all got something. You get what you get.*

"Yes, it's true, Emma," he says, repeating my line with a smile. "You get what you get."

Mom doesn't get the double entendre, not exactly. She doesn't understand that he's ribbing her, in that indirect guy sort of way. But she knows Fred means well, whatever he's saying. She's on the same vibrational wavelength, I imagine. And she knows, in her own way, that they are all — *we* are all — in this together, this long journey of "getting what we get." But she still glances over at Fred's diminishing stash of green Jell-O with a hint of jealousy.

19. *Shoo-flesh*

I once saw a man named Dexter give an astounding ping-pong exhibition. He was a patient at a psychiatric hospital. He didn't actually have classical psychiatric problems, more what you would call neurological problems; something not quite normal with the way chemicals worked in his nervous system. He was diagnosed with Tourette syndrome, the name for a collection of undiagnosable symptoms, and would make continuous, compulsive rapid-fire muscle twitches, like grabbing the end of his nose, or stretching his neck, or shrugging his shoulders. He was in constant motion, perpetually making semi-verbal sounds and half-articulating lyrics from songs and lines from movies. In addition, he would often exhibit coprolalia — an outburst of obscene words or socially inappropriate and derogatory remarks.

Although Dexter did not possess a repertoire of stable employable skills, one thing Dexter excelled at was playing ping-pong. He won nearly every game he played, even with Olympic-level champions, not so much because of his technical skill, but because of the astonishing speed and peculiar unpredictability of his serves and his returns. And when he had a chance to smash a shot — *squa-dooosh!* — he wouldn't just hit the ball hard enough to win the point, he would obliterate the ball with all his might, often causing it to hit the ceiling, or perhaps the chest or face of his opponent. And Dexter was known to gloat a bit whenever he won a point, sometimes belting out lyrics from show tunes: "Life is a cabaret, my friend" or "Don't cry for me, Argentina." This was already pushing the boundaries of sportsmanship, but occasionally he would go over the edge. At the end of a match, he might involuntarily resort to a crude slur as a way of exulting in his victory: "Beat the shit out of you, didn't I?" It was abrasive behavior like that which prevented Dexter from actually joining the professional tour.

Many of Dexter's opponents would give up after a few points, not able to take what they perceived to be verbal abuse or the humiliation of not being able to 'play their game.' Some would concede as early as during warm-ups, saying they were scared of Dexter. They simply couldn't understand his language, his way of relating to the world, his way of approaching the game, and this frightened them away. They never actually tried to break through.

Mom has two regularly assigned table mates for her meals. Fred is on her left, Sarah is on her right. In the same way that Dexter must have scared his opponents, Sarah frightens me. Oh, I know she's harmless physically. She's not brandishing a ping-pong paddle with machete-sharp edges and she's not wearing military fatigues with big black combat boots.

But it's the way she looks at me. I feel as if she knows my innermost secrets. *What are you hiding? What are you hiding? What are you so afraid of? Huh, what is it? Afraid you'll catch what I've got? You even know what I've got? Do you? Do you?*

Sarah always has an oxygen cartridge at her side, plastic tubes inserted into her nostrils. She breathes with an audible coarseness, an intensity that suggests each breath is charged with uncertainty. Sarah will occasionally make sudden moves with her head, torso, or arms.

She has a piercing intelligence about her and I notice her eyes racing about the room constantly.

Today, for the first time, I hear what sounds like words coming over the hissing of the oxygen valves. Her upper body heaves gently in rhythm with her breathing. She has her hand raised, like a junior high school student waiting to be called on.

Mom notices that my attention has shifted to Sarah. "She's a little off," Mom whispers, as she eyes Sarah sternly, leaning forward so only I can hear. Mom makes a little twirling motion with her right index finger near her right temple. I think she's trying to protect me from being sucked into Sarah's world.

Sarah does not hear Mom. I'm not sure if she hears anything that's coming from the outside world. She is now occupied with talking into her right hand in hushed tones as she makes little rotations with her raised left arm. "Sloo-fesh, all-fresh eat this what-do-they- think the fra-fre…" Her speech fades into silence, but her lips keep moving.

I try to engage Sarah's eyes to see if I can figure out what she wants. *Is Sarah neurologically impaired? Some kind of failure in the circuitry providing inputs from the cortex to the basal ganglia?*

Or is it me? Am I listening-impaired in not understanding her signs?

Save me! Save me! I imagine her saying. *Why am I being ignored like this?*

Fred seems to be reading my mind.

"She's just a little upset today," Fred says to me calmly. "She'll be fine."

He leans toward her. "You'll be all right, won't you, Sarah?" he says to her soothingly.

"Shoo-floooo," she continues.

An aide, Amanda, comes by, checking on how everyone is doing with their meals. She puts both hands on Sarah's shoulders and Sarah relaxes her arms to her side. Amanda leans in to speak to her. "Is there anything else I can get for you, love?" she asks, tapping her "r" sound in "there" and "for" in a charming Scottish brogue. "Don't you want to finish your juice, love?" she asks, bringing a glass of molten greenish liquid to Sarah's lips. Sarah calms for a moment and accepts a sip. Amanda pats her shoulders and moves on.

As soon as Amanda leaves, Sarah picks up the mantra, "Sh…fl…shooful," with her right arm hoisted again.

I am stuck, I am stuck in time, I imagine her pleading. And I start to feel with frightful vividness what it might be like to be imprisoned in this way permanently.

Increasingly, it sounds like Sarah is fuming, seething with rage. There's a growing urgency to her voice, a staccato rhythm to her pleas.

I turn to Fred. "What does she ha…?" I catch my gaffe. "I mean, what is her…?" No, that's not right either.

Fred smiles at me. He nods forgivingly.

"All of us have *something*," Fred says. He chuckles to himself, smiling inwardly.

All of us have something.

I look back at Mom. She has now forgotten about Sarah. She has forgotten about me talking with Fred. She has even forgotten about wanting dessert and is ardently scooping up a spoonful of her mashed potatoes.

Sarah's own efforts to emerge, to thrash her way into the consciousness of the others, have exhausted her. Her head has now dropped to the chest of her flowered gown, and she begins to nod in a peaceful sleep. I imagine her now, free and light, soaring above us.

You're no different from me, she seems to be saying, her words floating down like snowflakes. *We're all in this together. We're all in this together.*

136

20. My Best Friend

Klip-klop-klip-klop. Pause. "Hi, Howard." *Klip-klop-klip-klop.* Pause. "Hi, Jennifer. Good to see you." *Klip-klop-klip-klop.* Pause. "Hey, Lucy. How are you doing?"

I'm at Ellingwood, sitting in Mom's room, when Kate, my sister, drops in after work.

She greets Howard, the head nurse of the wing; Jennifer, one of the aides; and Lucy, a physical therapist.

You can always hear Kate coming up the hall, passing the nurses' desk and the atrium. Her chirping voice, the excited scurrying of people crowding around her to get a glimpse of her luminous cape as she glides gracefully down the polished linoleum hallway.

Kate greets the staff warmly, stopping to share jokes and pleasantries, hugs and handshakes and pats on the back.

She knows all the residents seated in the atrium and in the hallway and she greets them too, at least the ones who are awake.

Hi, Maggie, how are you doing today?

Hey, Fred. I love that sweater. Looking good.

Hi, Veronica. I've got something for you. I'll drop in on you later.

Kate enters Mom's room, carrying a stack of folded clothes. Mom is seated on her bed, leaning back into the large yellow pillow against the headboard. She looks up. I'm seated next to her, in the straight wooden 'guest chair.'

"Hi, Mom. How are you?" Kiss on the forehead. No affectionate greeting for me.

Mom is gathering herself and orienting to the new visitor in her room, but before Mom answers, she says, "I brought some clean clothes. You know that cute blue blouse you like so much. I found another one just like it…"

"Oh," Mom says, brightened by the vibrant energy Kate has brought with her. It's actually a healing energy — you will feel its potential if you're in her presence — though the effects aren't always immediately yielded.

Bump-boomp-bump-boomp. Once the clothes are in the drawers, Kate turns to Mom and picks up the white spiral-bound notebook from her bedside table.

"Let's fill in your diary, Mom," Kate says, as she sits on the edge of the bed.

Kate has only been here for a minute or so, and already this is more activity and more of a call to action than Mom usually receives in an entire day.

Mom stutters a bit, off guard, "O-o-h, I don't know if…"

Kate picks up the diary on the nightstand, leans into Mom and turns the page to today's date. "Who visited you today?" Display question.

"G-g-gabe," Mom says unprompted, though I *am* actually holding her left hand, hoping she gets this right. The tense doesn't matter: visit, visiting, visited, has visited, will visit, etc. It's all "visit." It's like the pidginization of a language: simplifying, simplifying, simplifying, in endless iterations, until everyone can understand.

"Let's write it in your diary," Kate says, sounding like a solicitous elementary school teacher.

I let go of Mom's hand. "Oh, oh, you write it for me," she says.

"Oh, you can write it today," Kate says, looking at Mom.

"Here, Mom, here's the pen. You can write it," I say, handing her the pen. I'm a bit skeptical, but I follow Kate's lead.

And Mom takes the pen, hand shaking. She writes slowly, but very legibly, and with perfect grammar, perfect spelling: *Gabe visits me today.*

Kate keeps building on. "And what did you do today?"

"Wait, wait, wait a minute," I say, not willing to cede the stage lights just yet. "And how do you feel about Gabe?"

"Who me?" Mom, says, puzzled. "Oh, I don't know."

"Well, I love you," I say. "Do you love me?" These are the kinds of direct things I could never say in Mom's pre-dementia days.

"Oh, of *course*, I do," Mom says. "I really *do* love you." And I believe her.

"Well, let's write that in the diary." I tap on the page with my index finger.

"I love Gabe." And hand shaking, she writes "I luve Gabe" on the next line. A small spelling error, but it will do. I'm genuinely moved. I don't think Mom ever said that to me directly before.

"My mother loves me! My mother loves me!" I gloat.

Kate rolls her eyes — *oh, puh-lease* — and puts the routine back on track.

"And what else did you do today?" Kate asks.

"Oh, I don't remember," Mom confesses. "It's been so long ago."

One of the new aides, Andrea, pops in to bring in some meds. Four little white paper Dixie cups with colorful little pills deposited on Mom's bedside table. Andrea notices Mom shakily writing in the journal. "What is she doing?" she asks quizzically.

"She's writing in her diary," Kate says very matter-of-factly.

"Oh, she can't write," Andrea replies. "She has Alzheimer's."

These must be the kinds of racist, sexist, ageist comments that people endure all the time in the guise of "Oh, I didn't really mean any harm by that, I don't know why you would be offended" explanations, but my hands begin to form a circle about the size of Andrea's neck. I resist the urge to strangle her. Kate just ignores this slight — she's tried in vain to win these little battles before — as the aide turns to leave with her meds cart, oblivious of having ruffled anyone's feathers.

After Mom completes her entries in the journal, Kate congratulates her: "Good job!"

Mom beams, like a fifth-grader bringing home an A on a math test.

"Why don't we take a walk in the garden?" I suggest. Kate translates this in Mom-speak: "It's such a lovely day out today and I just bet those petunias are in full bloom. Let's go out and say hello to them."

Mom quickly says, "Okay."

So, I help Mom into her wheelchair — she's not getting any lighter, I note — and wheel her outside. The three of us sit in the circular cobblestone area of the garden, Kate and I on a concrete bench facing Mom.

We're quiet for a while, then Kate poses a question, trying to start a conversation.

"Mom, do you remember all the traveling we did together? New Orleans, Boston, New York… We also went on a cruise in the Bahamas… with Sally and her mother."

Mom pauses, considering the thrust of the question: *people, places, together.* "I've kind of forgotten about that. That was before I got sick." In her more lucid moments, Mom divides her life into two periods: "before I got sick" and "after I got sick."

"We did a lot of traveling together. You've seen a lot of interesting places."

A major perk of Kate's work at Delta Air Lines was that she was able to travel virtually anywhere in the world for free, and bring a family member with her. Mom was most often the willing recipient.

"But we don't do that anymore," Mom points out, keeping up with the conversation admirably, and also making sure we grasp the underlying sadness of what she's saying.

Kate tries to refresh her memory, keeping the conversation lively. "The first place you and I went on a trip was to San Juan, Puerto Rico, just you and me. That was one of the best trips of my life."

Mom doesn't respond. The memory is not there. "I can't remember that. But was it a good time?" she queries.

"Oh, sure. You've had a lot of good times," Kate says buoyantly.

At that moment it became clear to me: *Kate is keeping Mom alive.* Physically. Mentally. Spiritually. She's preventing the library from burning down.

Kate reminds Mom of who she is, of what she has done, of what she loves and cherishes. Without Kate, I wonder if Mom would quickly shrivel up and fade away, with nothing to sustain her beyond the mushy meals and her medications.

Kate leaves after about an hour, an entourage of nurses and aides following her to the door, each getting a special personal message from Kate. I notice little smiles on the faces of the aides and nurses.

After Kate leaves — tough act to follow — I remain for a bit with Mom, wishing I had Kate's gift of being able to start conversations and carry them so fluidly. Of course, Kate must have learned all of this from direct apprenticeship with Mom, who in her day was famed for her ability to converse with anyone, anytime, anywhere, for any length of time. When I was a kid, I used to invent game shows that Mom would excel at: *How long can you talk to a stranger? How do you converse with someone who does not speak your language for ten minutes? How to retell stories, each time with a different ending?*

I say, "You're lucky Kate visits you every day, aren't you?"

"Yes, I guess so," Mom says, somewhat absently.

"And you know Kate talks so much. I wonder where she got that?" I say.

"Probably from me, I guess," Mom says, not missing a beat.

"Isn't it wonderful to have a daughter who loves you so much?" I say, a bit jealously.

Long silence. "Who?" Mom asks.

"Kate! Isn't it wonderful to have a daughter like Kate who loves you so much?"

"Oh, Kate's not my daughter," Mom scoffs, with a dismissive clucking sound.

"Sure, Kate is your oldest daughter," I say.

"No," Mom corrects me. "I have two daughters, but my daughters are much younger and much prettier," Mom adds, somewhat wistfully.

"Oh, really?" I ask, wondering how Mom thinks of them now.

"But I like Kate," Mom says, nodding. "She's my best friend. I don't exactly know *who* she is, or where she came from, but I know she's my best friend."

144

21. *Heartstrings*

One afternoon on a visit to Ellingwood, I saw a musician named Tami give an 'interactive concert' for a group of Alzheimer's patients. "It's not entertainment," she told me. "It's engagement. It's waking up the parts of the brain that are still working."

So she moves through her audience, transforming them from passive observers into participants. Once encouraged and guided, the members of the audience touch her guitars, harps and tambourines, eventually pawing them, stroking them, shaking them, fondling them, getting these instruments to make music. A few of the more mobile residents get on their feet to dance. I notice that Fred's wife, who was also visiting that day, has Fred on his feet, with her arms wrapped around him, doing a kind of salsa-bachata-saltero-minuet, or something. It doesn't matter what it is — you're moving and you're alive.

"Co-creating," Tami says. The smiles, the sparkles in the eyes, the swaying of the shoulders and hips, whatever we can touch — that's what we're going for.

"The parietal lobe," Dr. Patel had told us, "is always the last part of the brain to succumb." That's the part that is primarily involved in creativity.

"Humans have a remarkable ability to direct their energy into the parts of the body and the brain that serve them best," he said.

Yep, it's all about directing energy. Whenever I come to visit Mom now, I aim to have a strategy. I bring a game plan. X's and O's on the chalkboard, giving the team a pep talk before the big game. Ready, one-two-three game time. Whoop-whoop!

Inspired by Tami the Interactive Magician, I try to bring something to wake her up. Something to engage her. And yes, something to engage *me* also.

I'll show some photos. Mom has literally thousands of photos organized into little mini-albums, in piles in the basement of their house — and occasionally I'll bring a couple of them randomly to show her. Recently, it was an album with old photos of my little sister Charlotte.

The first picture is Charlotte in a pink tutu, about the age of five.

"Oh, who's that cute little girl? Is that Charlotte?" Mom asks, leaning in toward the picture.

"Yes, Mom, that's Charlotte." I say. "She's your baby." Charlotte is the youngest of her five children.

"Oh, she's wearing a…?" Mom has lost the word.

"A tutu. A pink tutu," I say.

"Oh, a *too-too*," Mom repeats slowly. That word's not part of the lexicon anymore.

"You made that for Charrie," I tell her.

"I did? I made that for Charlotte?" she asks, surprised. Then after a pause, "Oh, I did not! You're pulling my leg."

I remember the story, at least the version that Charlotte told:

Charlotte was *shattered* when Mom told her decidedly that she couldn't take ballet lessons — probably not in the family budget. Perhaps the request was a trigger from her own childhood when it was considered 'sinful' to want something for yourself that your siblings couldn't have. Mom herself had three brothers and five sisters, so wanting something just for yourself was *verboten, beschämend, schändlich.* Shameful.

But seeing Charlotte's crestfallen reaction, she did offer to fashion a tutu for her, out of some red tights and pink netting — among the hoarded treasures lying in wait in our basement — and kludged together a ballet outfit for Charlotte. It didn't look like a store-bought ballerina costume, but it worked just fine.

Leaning in closer to eyeball the picture, Mom says, "Oh, Charlotte looks so happy." Mom gently touches the girl in the picture with her fingertips. She asks, "Does she remember who *I* am?"

"Yes, Mom, she does. She thinks about you all the time."

"Oh, that's good," Mom nods. She's ready for the next picture.

Sometimes, after or instead of photo reminiscences, we'll take a walk in the garden and name the color of the flowers. Sometimes we'll do a ten-piece jigsaw puzzle of an elephant or a butterfly. And then we'll take it apart and put it back together again and again.

Sometimes we'll read rhymes and song lyrics and poems, repeating them over and over until it feels as if we're chanting ancient incantations. One of our favorites was from Edgar Allan Poe:

*I was a **child**, and she was a **child***

*In this **king**dom by the **sea***

*But we **loved** with a **love** that was **more** than a **love***

*I and my **An**nabel **Lee**...*

Eventually, after the third or fourth recital, we both stop saying the words and just make clucking sounds with our mouths in time with the rhythm.

Sometimes we'll look at art books, *The Medieval Books of Hours, The History of Italian Renaissance Art, Objects of Design*, gazing at art works, touching and talking to the pictures, marveling at the depth of human endeavor, commenting to each other about what we're seeing. *Spectacular. Outrageous. Calm. Lucid.* Or sometimes we'd just make up words. *Caclectic. Subonimal. Machesty. Granamolous.*

Sometimes I'll do 'chair yoga' with her. I'll sit in a chair in front of her and take the lead. She'll imitate, sometimes rotating her neck or her wrist slowly, absorbed in the transformative movements. She'll often make only a small mirroring of the movement, but it's the intention that counts! She loves hearing the names of the poses in Sanskrit: *upavista* or *virbadrasahna* or her favorite, *atmanjali mudra.* "Say it again," she'll request, and then smile. "Oh, that sounds so lovely." Shabda yoga.

Most of the time the chosen strategy doesn't work for long or doesn't work at all, but it's always worth trying *something.*

Today we're singing: "Let's sing a song today."

"Oh, I don't know how to sing."

"*Sure* you do. You're a natural. A regular Ella Fitzgerald. A Dinah Shore. A Doris Day."

Mom's eyes light up. She used to remind us that she went to the same high school as Doris Day — then Doris Kappelhoff — at Our Lady of the Angels in Cincinnati. The name seems to ring a bell, and her eyes roll upward in that "Oh, I know her" flash of recognition. "No, I'm not a singer like them."

"Oh, yes, you a-a-re. I know you." And I give her that Robert DeNiro two-fingers-to-the-eyes gesture: *I'm watching you.*

"Let's sing *Que Sera, Sera.*"

"I don't remember that."

I bet you do. It's a Doris Day song.

"I'll start…". I begin humming, and then start voicing the words.

Mom's eyes light up. She nods up and down, then smiles. And then she joins in, first with nonsense syllables, then words, and then occasionally full phrases.

She closes her eyes; her torso starts bobbing and she half-mumbles, half-sings along.

She starts tearing up. "Oh, this is making me cry."

"Oh, that's good!" I say. I've learned that tears have so many meanings. I'm not sure exactly what this round of crying means, but it feels cleansing and purifying.

We stumble through one more verse, making up words: *da dah Da-da-da…*

We pause now and breathe deeply, like marathon runners collapsing on the ground right after the finish line. *Pant, pant, pant.*

I notice I have my left arm around Mom's shoulders and we're holding hands with our right hands.

"You used to sing that to me when I was little," I tell her.

She looks up at me, her breathing more regular, full and deep now. *I did?*

"Yes, you used to sing it to me when I was getting ready for a nap. You'd lower the blinds and you'd sing that song. I'd even ask you what the song meant, and each time you made up a new story. Like once you said it means there's a secret sun, that you can only see when you're dreaming."

"I said that?"

"Yep, *un soleil caché*, can you see it? Can you see it? That means it's time to sleep."

"I did? I don't even know what *solo cachey* means."

"Sure you do. It's French," I say. "*Soleil caché.* You speak French, remember?" Mom used to boast about having straight A's in French in high school.

She beams proudly. "Oh, you."

Dolores, one of Mom's favorite aides, walks in and sees us holding hands.

"It looks like you and Emilie are having a heart to heart here," Dolores says.

"Yes, we've been singing," I say.

Dolores smiles. "Oh, she's a singer, aren't you, Emma?" Mom rolls her eyes, playfully punching at Dolores.

"Yes, it's one of her special talents," I say, nudging Mom's shoulder.

"Oh, you boys…"

Dolores continues, "She really knows how to pull everyone's heart strings, doesn't she?"

Mom closes her eyes, bathing in a peaceful internal bliss.

Sometimes the strategy works even better than expected.

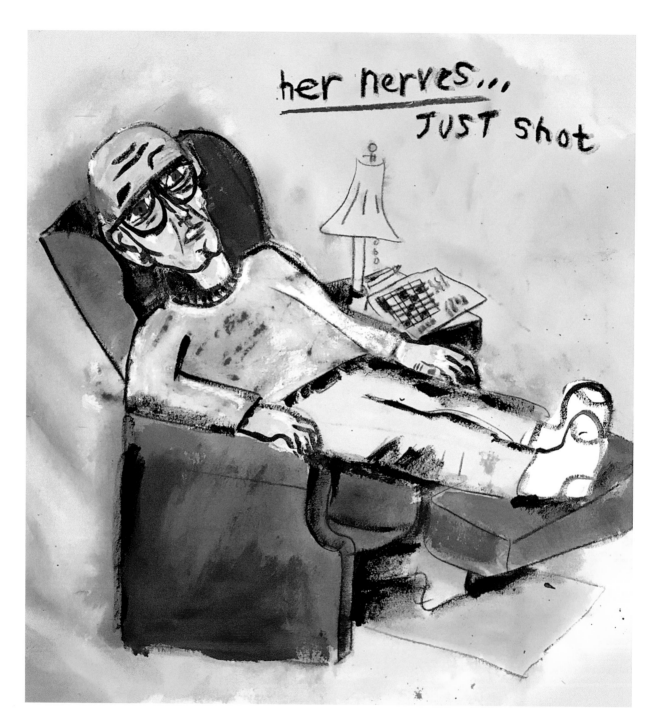

22. The Executive Report

Sunglasses, sunglasses, where did I leave my sunglasses? Damn, I must have left them on the dresser in Mom's room. I'll get them tomorrow.

I open the car door. It's about 200 degrees in there. I leave the door open for a minute to bring the temperature down to a tolerable level.

I slide into the driver's seat gingerly. I look at myself in the rearview mirror. Eyes drooping, cheeks hollow, mouth lax. I'm beat. It's been a draining visit.

As I start the car and wheel out of the parking lot, I consider stopping at Caribou Coffee. It's become my favorite contemplation spot in the neighborhood, especially if I need a bit of respite from Dad.

But I imagine Dad's now taking his afternoon nap, and I still have some freshly-ground coffee at his place, I recall. I picked up a pound of Kilimanjaro yesterday, a little burlap bag with a blue swishy logo of a reindeer on it. That'll do just fine. I can make a coffee and go down to the refrigerated basement and lick my wounds there.

I turn right off of Harrison Avenue onto Mitchell Place. I note how fast the drivers are coming in each direction. *Wheesh-wheesh-wheesh*, the parade of shiny silver Honda Accords, fiery red Ford F-150s, sleek black Chevy Malibus.

Man, they're coming fast and steady. It's clear now. Dad shouldn't be driving. His reflexes aren't fast enough for this kind of traffic. Next time he runs out for a pint of Graeter's Black Raspberry Chocolate Chip ice cream, he may never come back.

I pull up to Dad's house. Out of habit, I park flush with the right-hand side of the driveway, cognizant of one of Jake's Rules about always securing a quick exit. I've had my talk with Dad about how easy it is for me to move the car if he needs to get his car out, but this is just a variation of challenging the rule, and it got me nowhere.

I let myself in with my key. Standing in the foyer, it feels so quiet and cavernous here without Mom. It's her house, too. She's still here. Her fingerprints are still everywhere, on the design of the rooms, her choice of photographs to hang on the wall, her knick-knacks, her conversation pieces. Even her collection of refrigerator magnets stuck everywhere. *Welcome to Emma's Place.*

I assume Dad will be in his bed, but I see him dozing in his La-Z-Boy Zita Chair, now at a comfortable sixty-degree reclining position.

He looks up at me softly through half-closed eyes.

"How was The Mother?" he asks right away, in a dreamy voice barely loud enough for me to hear.

"She was very talkative," I say. I try to sound upbeat. Dad *craves* good news.

"That's good," he says. A slight smile comes across his lips. He's happy when I — or my brothers or sister — come from out of town to visit. We take over some of his self-imposed obligation to visit Mom every day. When we're not there, he visits Mom most days in the afternoon and Kate drops in at dinner time virtually every day.

But Dad enjoys reliving the visits *in absentia*— at least he wants to hear the highlights. Kind of like watching the sports highlight TV shows an hour after the game is over. So gratifying to re-experience the tiny victories.

I plop on the couch across from him and sit quietly for a moment. I plan how to frame my report. Maybe it's time now for "The Talk."

"Yes, she was very talkative today. But, you know, she's *really* tired," I say.

Dad opens his eyes a bit wider, interested. He raises his chair to a slightly more vertical position. This is Dad grammar: *I'm ready to listen.*

"I wanted to take a walk with her out in the garden after lunch, but she just wanted to go back to her room and take a nap."

"Ah," he says knowingly, adjusting his recliner to the full upright position.

"You know, I think *everything* is just getting tired." He looks at me quizzically.

"You know what I mean? It's not just her brain. It's her muscles. Her organs, too. Her heart, her lungs, her liver, her stomach…"

"Her nerves," Dad adds.

"Yeah, especially her nerves," I confirm.

"Just worn out," he repeats, his whole upper body nodding.

"Nothing wrong with that," I say. "Sometimes you just have to say, 'That's it. That's all I'm doing. I'm not doing anymore.'"

"Yeah," Dad nods. He's relieved. It's not exactly good news, like "She's so much better today." Not that kind of good news.

It sounds to him like a workable approach, a practical philosophy of life. *I've done my bit, and now I'm done. It's not my fault that I'm not going to live forever.*

He uses his remote control to lower his chair back to his dozing position.

"Guess what?" I pose cheerfully.

He looks at me wearily. He'd thought we were done with this conversation. "We sang a song. Guess which one."

"I have no idea."

"Que Sera, Sera."

Dad looks up into his brow, like he does when he's searching for a cue to a crossword puzzle.

"You know, that Doris Day song? You know that song, don't you?"

"Yeah, but I didn't know she knew it."

Of course he knew that she knew it. Blocking, the second sin of memory.

"Oh, yeah. She used to sing it to me often when I was little."

He gives me a puzzled look I realized then, that much of my childhood happened while Dad was at work.

"You know, before I started school, when it was just Mom and me at home, at nap time, we used to sing it together."

"I didn't know that," Dad says. Maybe he, too, is thinking, *Oh yeah, she is actually the one who raised my kids, isn't she?*

"We sang it again today. Her eyes really brightened up when we sang it. I told her that this was the '*sera*' part. The part you just can't predict. You just don't know how it's all going to end."

Dad seems to be tearing up a bit. *He's there, he's there! We're actually having The Talk!*

Dad closes his eyes. "I guess you just run out of *que*'s sometimes."

He nestles his back into the back rest and reclines his chair with a light jolt — *glu-glunck* — and soon begins his light snoring rhythm.

I tiptoe off to the kitchen to make my afternoon coffee. Yes, indeed, sometimes you do just run out.

23. *The Bath*

One of the mixed blessings of growing up in a staunch German Catholic family is that the family will entrust you to the reliable hands of religious educators. So when my father accepted a promotion to work in the Detroit office of Ford Motor Company, my parents first task was to locate reputable Catholic schools for the kids. I wound up enrolled in a Jesuit high school to begin high school.

One of the advantages of going to a traditional Jesuit high school was that I got exposed to some classics as an early teen, during my formative years. As a barely pubescent fourteen-year-old, I got to study ancient works like Plato's *Symposium*. Our freshman classics teacher, Dr. Huttinger, a crusty decorated World War II veteran who walked with a limp and had a reconstructed orange plastic ear, made us highlight passages in the book that we found particularly meaningful or puzzling.

I found myself highlighting passages about love, and then garnering the courage in the next day's class to read the passages aloud and ask for Hut's infallible interpretation. Passages like: *Love is simply the name for the desire and pursuit of the whole.* And, *The man who has been guided in the mysteries of love and who has directed his thoughts towards examples of beauty in due and orderly succession, will suddenly have revealed to him as he approaches the end of his initiation, a beauty whose nature is marvelous indeed, the final goal of all his previous efforts.*

Waking up today, I feel that I am nearing the end of my own initiation. I feel as much nervousness as I've ever felt before, before a high school tournament basketball game, before a final exam at university, before my first day of class at Lycée Tokoin in Togo, before a big conference presentation. Real stage fright, but the kind of stage fright you need to make a breakthrough.

This is the morning I'm going to give Dad a bath. It wasn't my idea actually. I had asked Kate if there was anything I could do while I was in Cincinnati on my current visit. I expected her to say something like clean the gutters, fix the leaky kitchen faucet, fell a tree, treat a snakebite. Something manly. Instead she said, "Yeah, give Dad a bath." While she had been doing virtually every support task imaginable, from arranging Dad's appointments, to washing his clothes, to discussing Mom's progressive Alzheimer's, she didn't feel comfortable bathing him.

To get Dad to do anything new is a gradual, iterative, circuitous process of persuasion. You must somehow satisfy him that what you're planning to do is: (1) in his best interest; (2) that it absolutely needs to be done; and trickier still (3) that it needs to be done at the time you're proposing doing it. I started the first persuasion goal a day earlier, talking about how Kate had suggested it, that having me help would be safer for him, that it wasn't a burden on me to do it.

He was gradually buying into it, as long as I kept repeating it as if it was a regular activity that he did all the time. Deliberate practice, we call this in applied linguistics.

Achieving the second goal was going to be more elusive because he could always find a counter argument to the absolute necessity of any action. His own sense of being forced to do something was reason enough to deny its necessity. So it was important to get him to feel that it was *his* idea that it needed to be done. I had to slip in at least one, "Do you still really want me to give you a bath tomorrow?"

And then achieving third goal put you on the level of an Edmund Hillary or Ernest Shackleton: so many reasons to give up before you reach the summit. Dad could always find a way to put off the agreed activity up to a moment before it happened. There was no way to prepare for all of the possible diversionary ploys he would muster at the last minute. I tried a tactic that had worked a few times in the past: game planning. So I set a time — 7:30 a.m. — and walked through the individual actions together.

We did virtual rehearsals of the event several times: *I'm going to wake you up at 7:30. You're not going to put in your contact lenses, okay?* Dad had had a cataract operation years earlier, before the technology had advanced to allow for implants, and needed to insert contact lenses to see properly. Once he put them in for the day, he would not remove them until he went to bed at night. *And then we're going to...*

Dad is definitely not comfortable with this style of decision making. There was no way that *anyone* under the age of eighty — not some pipsqueak who hadn't earned his stripes — was going to boss him around.

But I know if I don't outsmart him somehow, he's going to dig into his bag of excuses to put this off indefinitely. *I'm not sure this is a good idea. I'd rather wait. The cleaning lady is coming tomorrow. I don't want to do it while she's here.*

Dad, we've already discussed this. We're getting up at 7:30. We'll take a shower then. We'll be done in 15 minutes, before 8 o'clock. Nancy is coming at 10. He looks at me funny, as if my calculations on this are way off.

So the morning of the big dance has arrived. I've done my best to prepare. Let's just hope I can pull this off.

Heading up to the kitchen, I peek into Dad's room. He's already out of bed. Damn! I tap on his bedroom door and peer around the corner. He's in the bathroom, opening and closing drawers in the vanity.

"*Morning, Dad*," I shout. He turns and looks at me, seemingly surprised to see me.

"Are you ready for your shower?" I ask cheerfully.

He looks alarmed as I walk up to him. "I haven't eaten anything yet."

"That's fine," I assure him. "We'll shower first, then you can eat."

"But I can't find my contact lenses," he says with a note of desperation in his voice.

"Oh, we'll find them after we take your shower," I tell him calmly. "You don't want to put them in before you take your shower."

I guide him into the bathroom. He turns around sternly. "But I really want to know where my contacts are first," he announces firmly.

"I'll tell you what," I say in my best negotiation tone. "You go into the bathroom and get undressed, and I'll find your contact lenses. I promise." He looks up at me, a bit defeated, then sits down reluctantly on the toilet lid to take off his socks.

I go down to my bedroom and return with the two round contact lens cases. I had hidden them the night before after he went to bed. *Sorry, Dad.*

Stepping into the bathroom, I deftly place the contact case silently back into the sink drawer, and announce, "Oh, here they are." Dad pops up from the toilet seat in disbelief. "Here they are," I repeat. "Your contact lenses. They were…*mumble mumble.*"

He looks at me, sighing with disbelief.

Resigned, Dad sits back down and continues to undress.

In a few minutes, there he is, unclothed and ready. He's standing, nude, hunched forward, holding on to the wall bar with his left hand. Muscled arms and shoulders, firm thighs and calves: an aging athlete. Then a small mass of clay-like flesh, folding toward the middle, undefined, mysterious. His stooped body creates an aura of magnificence, of nobility.

Putting my arm on his back to guide him toward the tub, I notice his feet. They resemble the fierce talons of a hawk, clutching at the linoleum floor. Red and raw, his feet arc in an outward spiral away from the center, ankles thick as the roots of an aged oak. Stooped by his feet, I caress his right ankle, feeling its puffy softness. "These feet have done a lot of marching," I note.

Detecting a note of pity in my voice, he provides one of his customary attitude adjustments: "Well, I haven't exactly been floating these past eighty years."

Letting go of his ankle, I look again at his feet. They seem to defy the laws of physics, appearing to be simultaneously above *and* below the surface of the floor.

I help Dad step over the side of the tub. He pulls his legs upward one at a the time and sets them down like a sumo wrestler, plop-plop, on the floor of the bath. I help him lower toward a white plastic seat in the middle of the bath. Once he is in front of the seat, we slowly settle his torso down, down, down onto the white stool. Only now do I breathe a sigh of relief. He can't escape.

"Start the water," he directs me from his command stoop, head down. Kneeling on the other side of the tub wall, I pull the faucet forward, gradually rotating the knob toward the right temperature. We both know Dad is not going to be satisfied — will decide *not* to be satisfied — until the fourth or fifth adjustment, so I might as well start off at a ridiculously cold setting.

"Too cold!" he admonishes loudly, as I test the water on the back of his right hand. "Still too cold. Now it's too hot. No, too cold. Okay, that's okay." He waves his hand in surrender.

"Are you ready?" I ask. He nods almost imperceptibly. "Then let's start with your arms."

He raises his left arm, and holding it from the underside, I spray the nozzle over the arm, then give it to him to hold. I begin soaping the arm with a liquid soap 'for cleaning micro pores' that I bought at Walgreens the night before. I use both hands, massaging the soap around, from his wrist to his arm pit, again and again.

"How does that feel?" I ask. His head is bowed now. He doesn't hear me. I repeat on the right arm, noting his wiry muscle tone. Are these the same arms that used to fungo-bat baseballs to me high into the sky so that I could practice catching pop-ups? They are so thin now, probably unable to launch the baseball beyond the rooftops anymore.

I continue to his back. I place my hand on the forest of graying hair, the constellation of moles and imperfections on his skin — all of which I have inherited from him. I glide the warm water over his shoulders. With the cumulative warmth of the water, he gradually relaxes his entire torso. His chest sags inward and he coughs and gasps a bit. I massage the soap over his upper back and rinse in a circular motion.

For a moment, he seems to melt into my hands. "Does that feel good?" I ask.

He doesn't answer, but I can tell that it does.

So here I am, giving my aging father a bath for the first time. I don't care what others may call it, this is "the desire and pursuit of the whole." I have been guided in the mysteries of love.

24. The Fall

Kaboom! The entire house vibrates.

"Dad, are you all right?" My brother Liam rushes up from the downstairs bedroom. Liam has been staying with Dad for the past several days. It's two a.m., Dad is lying on the floor next to his bed, flat on his back, staring at the ceiling. He's whimpering in pain.

"Are you okay?"

"Yeah, I'll be okay," Dad groans. "Just help me get back into bed."

"Maybe we ought to go to the ER," Liam says, helping him up.

"No, I'll be fine. Just get me back into bed," he orders irritably. With Liam's help, he contorts himself back into bed and Liam covers him with the bed sheet.

From about the time of our visit to the Greenview Café, Dad's physical health had begun to decline. His balance, vision, appetite, and his memory were all waning.

He started moving increasingly slowly, taking more time to get into and out of chairs. After a couple of slips on the ice during the winter, he finally agreed to use a cane for walking.

First thing the next morning, Liam goes into Dad's room to ask him how he is.

Dad acts confused. "I don't know what happened. My back is aching all over."

"You fell last night," Liam reminds him.

"I did?" he says. "Don't remember." Bias — one of the sins of memory. Liam has to make note of this, to tell the doctor. That's got to be a sign of…*something.*

Liam takes Dad to Hamilton North Hospital, carefully guiding him into the car, maneuvering him into a wheelchair and steering him into the emergency room. A little paperwork, not too bad. They ask how Dad fell. Liam, the consummate engineer, does a quick calculation and decides on a benevolent white lie: *He slipped on the bathroom floor*. If they think he fell because he was dizzy or disoriented, they'd probably want to do brain scans. Liam decides, *Nah, we don't need to go there*.

Like Dad, Liam has an inherent distrust of the medical establishment, not because they're incompetent, but because they're *overly* competent. By the time they exhaustively discover all of the diagnostic information they need, something else will have occurred to complicate matters. An endless chase for the truth, when, in the current timeframe, the truth doesn't matter. *We just need a quick fix for his back. We'll take it from there.*

They take him downstairs for X-rays. A burly male nurse nudges Liam aside and assumes the navigator position. Dad seems to like the royal treatment. Being wheeled around by a professional is kind of nice!

All in all, pretty efficient. After a short wait, a nurse calls Liam into an examination room. Dad is already there with the nurse standing to the side of his wheelchair.

Liam moves around to the other side of the wheelchair, running his fingers across the top of the aqua blue plastic chair before sitting down. *Hmm, polyethylene terephthalate*, he notes. A wizard chemical engineer, Liam understands the composition of *everything* in the known universe. We used to call him our family's walking library, and later "Lia-pedia," for his endless wellspring of knowledge.

A young doctor in a short Cherokee white lab coat bursts into the room and greets them. "Hi, I'm Dr. Matus." He shakes Liam's hand politely. Dad doesn't look up. He sits down at his mobile desk, wheeling it around to face Dad. He quickly punches up the X-ray pictures on his computer. Assuming a meditative position, he examines the slides, leaning forward to study the details.

Turning the computer screen so both Dad and Liam can see it, he announces, "It looks like you fractured a couple of vertebrae, Mr. Bron." Liam leans forward to examine the X-rays, but Dad doesn't show much interest in the medical details. "How do you feel?" he asks, projecting his voice toward Dad.

Dad knows the doctor is now addressing him. "Like a bayonet is prodding me in the back," he mutters, in a guttural barking sound. The doctor smiles empathetically. He doesn't understand the vague reference Dad has tossed in about the Bataan Death March, one of many war experiences my father never delves into. The doctor is young enough to be his grandson. The Second World War would be beyond '*zamani*' for Dr. Matus: false memories, fantasies, caprices, stories *old* people tell. But he nods reassuringly, in appreciation of my father's attempt to communicate.

"It must really hurt. Back pain can be very severe," he says. Liam wonders if this is true empathy or just part of the ER protocol. *Ah, why not give him the benefit of the doubt?*

Dad nods silently. He's not giving anybody any benefits.

The doctor smiles. "Well, the *good* news is nothing is *broken*. But the bad news is there's not much we can do here, except give you a wrap, send you home and ask you not to make sudden moves for a while. And we *can* give you some medication to help with the pain." He holds up a fist-sized bottle of hydrocodone, dangling it before him like a houseowner might tempt trick-or-treaters with Halloween candy.

"Medication? Oh, hell, no!" Dad broadcasts, this time clearly articulating every word. He decides to commandeer control of the visit. This is after all, about him.

Dr. Matus smiles graciously. "Well, we'll see how you do."

"I guess this means you have to put your ping pong game on hold for a while," Liam quips, trying to lighten the mood.

Dad is not amused.

"Will it heal?" Liam asks the doctor.

"Well, little fractures can take a long time to heal, especially at your father's age," Dr. Matus says matter-of-factly.

Dad eyes Dr. Matus suspiciously. *At your father's age?* This sounds like code for *No, it will never heal.*

Liam is willing to accept this assessment. A lot of things never heal, he knows that. But he wants to explore the options. "So that's it?"

"Well, I can discuss some options with *you*, if you like." Liam takes this as signal that maybe it's best if Dad is not present for the next part. "Let me wrap this first," the doctor replies. He exits to fetch the Pro-Tec wrap for Dad.

Liam calls Kate at work to give a quick update. Kate is ready with a Plan A and Plan B. She's already thought this through. Liam nods, "Um-hmm. Um-hmm. Okay, got it. I'll let you know."

Dr. Matus re-enters the room almost as soon as Liam finishes his call with Kate. He's holding the wrap, ready to work. Dad seems to know the drill and pulls up his shirt and looks away toward the corner of the room. The doctor pulls the wrap around him snugly and seals the Velcro.

"Too tight?" he asks him.

"A little," Dad grunts.

Scooch, adjusts, grunt, *scooch*, adjust, *fwwwwp*. "How's that?"

"Yes, that's fine," Dad responds. "Thank you.*"*

Thank you? Dad actually said that? Expressing gratitude is an obscure sub-category in Jake's rulebook, something only the masters dare engage in, and then very sparingly.

Liam nods to the attending nurse that he can handle things from here. "Dad, why don't you sit out in the waiting room. I've got some details to take care of here." Liam wheels Dad to the waiting room.

There's a replay of the previous night's Reds versus Phillies game on the TV bolted to the wall. Dad leans back into his chair.

Liam ducks back behind the curtain. Dr. Matus pulls himself away from his computer screen.

"Oh, yes, Mr. Bron, just a couple of things I'd like to go over with you.*"* Liam decodes the euphemism as a sign that things aren't all rosy.

"First, I noticed on his X-ray that his lungs have some irregularities. You probably know this?" he probes.

Liam shrugs. "Well, yes, at his age and all, the history of smoking. Not surprising."

"We could explore that, do some imaging, maybe a sputum cytology and see if there's something..."

Don't want to go there, Liam is thinking, as he shakes his head politely. "Maybe that's something we can monitor for the time being?" he offers.

Dr. Matus understands. "Yes, if nothing's really bothering him, there's no point in these painful diagnostic procedures."

So he admits it: Diagnosis can be painful.

"Well, let me know if it gets any worse. As for his back," he continues, "we can give him some hydrocodone for the pain, if you like. I know he said that he'd prefer not to…"

It takes Liam all of a microsecond to process the implications of this idea. "No, let's not do that. Not right now."

"Okay, then, well, I think your father is ready to go home." Turning point.

Liam puts on his negotiator cap. "I was wondering if you can tell him that it's best if he recuperates at Ellingwood."

This is Kate's Plan B. Dad couldn't possibly return home and be by himself. He couldn't move around. He would be in pain. He wouldn't have anyone to complain to. He would likely fall again.

Kate had already reserved a room in the independent living wing of Ellingwood for Dad as a stop-gap measure.

"Sure, I can do that," the doctor offers. The tension mounts. Drum roll. *Duunnn dunnn… duuuunnnn duun…*

How will Dad respond to this idea?

Dr. Matus comes out into the waiting room with Liam and walks over to Dad who's glued to the television. It's now the fourth inning — Ground Hog's Day, he watched this same game last night — and the score is tied three to three. High drama.

"Mr. Bron, your son and I were discussing the best options for you, to help you recuperate. We were thinking that it might be best if you spend some time at…"

Liam completes the sentence. "Ellingwood." Then he adds, "Just until your back starts to feel better."

Epiphany. Moment of catharsis.

Dad sighs deeply. Maybe watching the baseball game gave him some time to think things through. He nods. "You know, maybe you're right."

A moment of clarity, another benefit of baseball, the perfect game.

Part Four: Coming Home

Home From The War

Lizard Den

Curtain Call

The Transition

The Vigil

The Promise

The Day After

Winter Jasmines

Silver Stockings

Six White Horses

Rasa Yatra

25. *Home from the War*

We often think of our lives as linear, starting with birth and proceeding chronologically through a sequence of events until it's all over. We remember things forward and backward. In relation to what came before and after.

Maybe that's the schema we have hardwired into our brains. But I think the way we experience life is more like an untimed series of pulses in a pond, rippling outward. In the world of dementia, memory is more like a re-experiencing of pulses, seemingly random pulses, interacting with other pulses, some stronger, some weaker.

For both of my parents, the strong pulses originate certainly from the spartan realities of their childhood, from their courtship, from the war. Especially from the war, going off to war, fearing you may never be reunited, then finally reuniting, those pulses are particularly strong.

Following Dad's fall, Kate made a call to Ellingwood. She wanted to reactivate her earlier request for Dad to try out an apartment in the 'independent living' wing. This was a gentle plan to get Dad to give up his house, with all of the responsibility of taking care of it, and all of the danger of him falling. Even with declining cognitive abilities, Dad could easily read between the lines, and understood what moving out of the house would mean. It would mean giving up the dream of Mom getting better and moving back in with him, a kind of "happily ever after" fantasy he had been holding onto in private.

Kate thought that Dad would *surely* qualify for 'independent living,' even with limited mobility after his fall. He was, after all, this strong man who had done so many powerful things in his life, who had, who had, who had...

Not anymore.

During the admission interview, Dad failed the mobility tests, first off. He couldn't turn his torso more than thirty degrees and he couldn't bend down to pick something up from the floor. He couldn't move his arms above shoulder height. And then of course, he made these ungodly groans with the attempted compliance with each of the 'test items.' How on earth was he to live alone?

To Kate's disappointment, he also failed the cognitive tests — *uh-oh!* For Kate, who had been seeing Dad every day for the past year, it was the 'boiling frog' syndrome. Sure, his cognitive abilities were declining — aren't everyone's? — but oh-so-gradually.

And then finally — no surprise to Kate — he failed the communication tests: the mini-cog test and the verbal fluency tasks.

But wait... When did this all happen? Yes, the frog gradually gets used to the increasing temperature of the boiling water until it's too late to jump out of the pot.

The three staff members in attendance unanimously determined that Dad flunked all three tests — mobility, cognition, communication — and needed to be in the *full-time* nursing care unit. Independent living would be like buying a condo in Cabo San Lucas. *No, not going to happen.*

At least not for now. That's the euphemism in the nursing world for "Don't even think about it."

Howard, the senior nurse, calls Kate and Dad into the nursing office. Kate wheels Dad into the room. Dad is still in a wheelchair, as he's been ever since the ER visit. He seems to like the attention and the instant alleviation of his role as the main decision-maker. Salvation at last!

It doesn't take long for Howard to get to the point. "Mr. Bron, considering all the circumstances, I think it's best if you move into full-time nursing care... *for the time being,*" he advises. There's that euphemism routine again.

Dad is quiet, looking down at the floor solemnly. He has accepted his fate, but it is still shocking to hear someone pronounce it for you.

Kate is calm. She has seen in her crystal ball for some time what the eventual ending would look like. "Yes, Dad, it's just for... you know, until... we can decide what..." She doesn't have a way to put it just now that will connect with Dad's conception of time.

Howard smiles. "And, Mr. Bron, the good news is..." He waits for Dad to take a guess at what the good news is.

Dad is starting to enjoy the game-like quality of the event, but his back still hurts. He doesn't want to play. "I don't know. Tell me," he whispers.

"Your roommate will be Emma!" he announces, invoking his inner Alex Trebek.

Howard explains that they recently had a couple of 'openings' on the floor. This is another euphemism, this one for residents passing away. Nobody *decides* to move out of Ellingwood, say, to a condo in Cabo or a mansion in Nassau. Given the changes in 'the resident roster,' they could move Veronica across the hall and have Dad move in with Mom, in Room 103. Howard has it all worked out.

Dad nods. Another ripple in the pond. *Yes, this all makes sense. What else could have possibly happened?*

Kate is pleased with Dad's reaction. She looks at him with an air of triumph — worthy of a grand high-five, except that this gesture isn't really part of their interaction system, and Dad's back hurts too damn much to lift his arm.

Kate moves Dad's things into room 103, where the name plate *Daniel B.* is already placed on the door, *above* Mom's *Emma B.* In her prime, Mom might have cocked her head and said, "Oh, that's kind of patronizing. Sexism aside, I was here first, after all."

Kate, with her complex network of friends and affiliates, had someone from work with a pickup bring Dad's suede recliner, and the basket full of partially-completed crossword puzzle books he kept next to it. He didn't really need much else. There was already a TV in the room.

"Anything else you need from home, we can bring it right away," Kate promises him.

Mom watches the move taking place, like someone watching the ending of *Casablanca* for the nineteenth time. *You know what's going to happen.* Veronica, her long-time roommate, has been moved across the hall. Mom is visibly sad as she watches Veronica being wheeled away. She has seen a number of people leave and never come back.

Dad comes lumbering in slowly, using his cane now, a sign that he's on the mend, or at least he wants to be perceived as being on the mend. He's actually in a great mood, in spite of the backache. He's whistling an aria from the opera *Carmen*.

He doesn't know what the words are, but the dramatic harmonization seems right for the occasion.

"Hello, The Mother," he says. He's been calling her "The Mother" for years now. "I'm home."

Dad may be trying to conjure up those golden days when he'd pull his tan Ford Falcon into the driveway after a day at the office, open the screen door, and say in his best *Father Knows Best* voice, "Honey, I'm home."

Mom seems to pick up on this, as if he were returning home at precisely 5:45 and she was stirring a pot of chili on the stove. "Hi, dear," she says.

That night, around two a.m. Mom wakes up and looks over to the other side of the room where she expects to see Veronica sleeping. Instead, she notices a man sleeping soundly, snoring lightly.

She squints over at him. *Who is this? What is he doing here?* she thinks, looking over at her new roommate.

Then, *wait, wait!* she thinks gleefully. *I know him. I know this person.*

She sits up in bed and fumbles with the pitcher of water and the clock next to her bed, feeling for the large desk phone. Somehow, she remembers this routine, picking up the receiver, and pushing the buttons on the huge dial. She hasn't used the phone in several months, but it was always there as a reminder that she *could* call outside if she wanted to. She punches the numbers of Kate's cell phone one by one, her number posted in big figures on the wall by her bedside.

Kate is asleep, hears her cell phone buzzing, and picks it up slowly.

"Kate! Kate!" Mom shouts excitedly. "You won't believe this."

"Mom? Mom! Is that you?" Kate says, a bit groggy. The last time Mom tried using the phone was months ago.

Mom continues, bubbling, "Your father is here. Your father is here! Your father has come home from the war!" The pulse of memory, which had weakened and practically threatened to disappear in the cloud of dementia, was revitalized! *He's here, he's here, he's home at last!*

26. *Lizard Den*

When my son Christopher was about ten, I went to the Vivarium in Berkeley with him to pick out a pair of lizards for a school science project. The herpetologist on duty, Starr, a young woman with a network of purple spiderwebs tattooed across her shoulders and down her arms, interviewed us extensively to make sure we would be suitable as 'shepherds' for the pair of Argentine black-and-white tegus we had picked out. First, we had to show her detailed photos of where the lizards would live. Then we were asked a series of screening questions starting with: *Have you or has anyone in your family ever exhibited a phobia of reptiles?* When we passed — or lied our way through — the interview, we were allowed to fork over two hundred and fifty dollars to take home Lizzie and Sheldon.

Starr told us that it would take the lizards about a month ("twenty-eight to forty-two days") for the pair to get accustomed to living together, to realize that they needed to adapt to each other, to get along in confined quarters, and to give each other 'appropriate space.' During this time, they would actually alter the physical pattern of the spots on their scales to accommodate their mate and also adjust their sleeping and eating patterns, movements, and even their breathing patterns to match the other.

"These things take time," Starr counseled us. "There's no way to rush the process." She gave me her card, imploring me to call her "any time of day or night" if the lizards showed any sign of "distress" adapting to their new home. And there was a full money-back guarantee if we decided we were simply not able to care for them properly.

There was no money-back guarantee if Mom and Dad did not get along in their new shared habitat, but they had previously had some sixty years to perfect their mutual adaptations. Although they were limited physically and mentally, they eventually fell back into a familiar rhythm.

Dad, now free of the daily obligations of running his life and worrying about Mom, started to resemble a college kid on spring break. Just as you might go for a few days without shaving when you're on holiday, you might go for several weeks without any sort of serious thinking or problem solving when you're in an institution. Dad was starting to realize: Hey, this institutional thing is not so bad.

Just as Mom had become stronger with the calm routine of Ellingwood, Dad also seemed to begin healing after a few weeks. He began moving a bit more fluidly, started doing crossword puzzles, started watching *Jeopardy* and *Wheel of Fortune* during the day. Kate had brought his blue suede chair to his new room and he seemed to be back in his element.

Mom was still exhibiting all of the classic symptoms of Alzheimer's, now clearly in the 'moderate' stage:

- Being forgetful of events or personal history.
- Feeling moody or withdrawn, especially in socially or mentally challenging situations.
- Being unable to recall information about herself like her address or telephone number.
- Experiencing confusion about where she is or what day it is.
- Requiring help choosing proper clothing for the season or the occasion.
- Experiencing changes in sleep patterns, such as sleeping during the day and becoming restless at night.
- Showing an increased tendency to wander and become lost.
- Demonstrating personality and behavioral changes, including suspiciousness and delusions or compulsive, repetitive behavior like hand-wringing or tissue shredding.

Of course, Mom would have occasional good days, when she'd show minimal signs of any of these symptoms. On those days, she would actually thrive — interacting easily, participating actively, recalling names and places readily.

These were inevitably followed by bad days, where she would exhibit *all* of the symptoms. Check, check, check, check, check.

Most disturbing to visitors was when she was unable to recognize people or recall things they had in common or seemed to be unwilling to participate in any conversation. It turned out that many of her former visitors, old neighbors, nephews and nieces, and even once-close friends, simply stopped coming, unable to cope with 'the new Emma.'

Mom and Dad themselves didn't converse much during their time together. They didn't need to. And they certainly seemed comfortable — comforted really — being in each other's presence. And they always shared a good night kiss, with Dad hobbling over to her bed, and leaning down for the smooch. *Good night, Emilie.*

It wasn't always clear that Mom knew who Dad was. She once said to him after one goodnight kiss, "I don't know who you are, but I really like you."

It was pure magic. Wait — I think there's a movie here! Hollywood pitch: Boy meets girl, boy falls in love with girl, due to tragic events, girl forgets who boy is, boy plots how to re-enter girl's life with a new identity. *What do you think, Sidney? Got a winner here?*

Around this time, sustaining a conversation with Mom was becoming increasingly challenging. Conversations typically fizzled out after one or two exchanges.

Kate hit upon the perfect low-stress form of continual communication: the oral word puzzle. Kate would read out a clue, like "A river between Cincinnati and Covington," four letters, and the puzzlers would shout out their answers. If Mom was stuck, additional clues of any sort would often trigger her memory and she'd blurt out the answer. "Ohio!" We'd all applaud, even Dad, who learned to hold back shouting out the correct answer as soon as he knew it.

Phatic communion. Who knew crosswords, long a *divider* between Mom and Dad — "How can he even hear me? He's doing one of his crossword puzzles?" was one of her frequent grievances — would become their new *uniter*. It would become a new lingua franca, a shared code. Each clue was a brand new conversation, *intentionally* unconnected to the previous clue.

Even if Mom wasn't always able to follow the clues, she was generally on top of the game, knowing what was going on, and sometimes even asking the score — which Kate would usually just make up.

The clues and the responses weren't always what you'd expect.

Kate poses the clue: "City built on seven hills." Pregnant pause. "Four letters." Her inner Alex Trebek is blossoming.

"Rome," Dad spurts out quickly, too late to be shushed by Kate or me.

"Cin-cinn-a-ti," Mom says. She says it a bit shakily, but very confidently, four syllables in a rhythmical cadence.

"That doesn't have four letters," Dad replies. "She said, four letters."

Kate frowns at Dad's insistence on adhering to the rules.

"C-I-N," Mom says. "...N."

Dad looks up, massaging his lower lip with his teeth. Unlike he had been in his pre-reptilian life, Dad is slowly learning to be patient with Mom during these games, trying to wait for her to take a stab at the answer before he'd chime in. Years earlier he might have called her response "cockamamie" and jumped in with a corrective riposte, but now he smiles pleasantly, gives a thoughtful nod of recognition.

I suppose she's forgotten that Cincinnati is a Shawnee word for "seven hills." But I'm sure she remembers that she has been to the top of each of those seven hills.

The game clock was off. Correct answers are not the point. Scoring was arbitrary.

The crossword activity would work for a while, but of course it wasn't a panacea. If Mom was having a bad day, she wouldn't want to play or would tune out immediately. Often, in the middle of a game, Mom would get upset and blame Dad for something out of the blue: *What is wrong with him? He never pays attention to me.*

Dad would look up and shrug, usually with an impish smile. Translation: *That's just her way of communicating.*

Life in the lizard den.

ITS
TIME.

27. Curtain Call

Today is the day I've promised to take Dad out to lunch, a break from the normal 'healthy' Ellingwood cuisine. The dietician on duty knows we 'skip school' like this from time to time and are likely to indulge in some unhealthy lunch choices, but she also knows the benefits of feeling free and even whimsical decision-making. "Bon appetit!" she says cheerfully as we slowly move past the nurses' station toward the parking lot.

I somehow know that today's lunch fling out on the town will involve more than just eating. I can sense that Dad is struggling with the reality that he may never be able to return to their home, they will at some point need to 'give it up.' Still, though, he fully intends to be able to go back for a visit from time to time, 'since we're in the neighborhood.'

Just as my mother had her episode of 'giving up games' at Bridge Night, my father had his own 'throwing in the towel' experience with his former life. Dad's resignation was from his starring role in his own production of "The Office." Dad played his role of home-life manager with focus and purpose, a one-man show without a supporting cast, and with only one major prop — the lion's share of the dining room table converted into his own version of "Office Space."

Before his fall and admission to Ellingwood, Dad used to sit down periodically at the massive table in the middle of the dining area, and systematically work his way through the stacks of papers, bills and notices that had accumulated. It was an awesome show. There was a time when he could buzz through an amorphous heap of correspondence in thirty minutes, leaving an aftermath of neat piles of papers and precisely-opened envelopes, with a pad of neatly written notes on his 'action points.' His mainline approach to paperwork, one that he taught me when I was a teenager, was "if you touch something, improve it, act on it, or move it forward. Don't just put it back in the pile." That was the 'systems guy' we had all come to expect to sleuth through any problem, no matter how complex, and — come hell or high water — arrive at a solution. There was a time when he was a master of his world.

But over recent years, that disciplined approach had begun to dissolve. Dad now avoided scheduled trips to his workspace and once seated, he was now given to picking up and reshuffling papers without doing anything about them, often sighing hopelessly as he tossed another incomprehensible page onto the pile.

In his last few months at home, Dad started insisting that we make copies of everything, "just to be sure I don't lose it. Can you make copies of this?" he would ask, proffering a sheaf of papers if I headed out of the house for any reason. I had thought of getting him his own copy machine, but then reconsidered. That would clearly be enabling, kind of like handing a liquor store gift card to an alcoholic.

At first, Kate would accommodate Dad, as a way of humoring him really, and letting him know that she cared that he was trying to stay on top of things, but now his need for backups had spiraled out of control. There were multiple copies of virtually everything: contracts with Ellingwood, tax forms, Medicare forms, retirement accounts, letters announcing reunions, news clippings, obituaries, notices, advertisements. Copies of receipts from Copy Central.

I tried to explain how, with digital technology, we could now make electronic copies of everything and safely store them, but he always looked at me suspiciously when I said this. *Who can trust that?*

Now that Dad had moved into Ellingwood, and the weeks have slipped by mercifully without any impending audit from the IRS or an overdue payment notice from Duke Energy, it's sinking in that he may *never* need to return to the turmoil — and the persistent memories — that the office table represents. Maybe angels somewhere will take care of it all with the sweep of a wand, or maybe, like the weekly game of bridge, just refusing to play anymore is all that is needed to end the game.

Today is the day I've promised to take Dad out for lunch and possibly a sneak back into the old palace.

Dad has been at Ellingwood for about three months, and he's still mobile enough and energetic enough to go on short outings. He uses a walker, a foldable Invacare model with wheels that I can easily fit into the back of the car.

As we make our way through the glass doors out to the parking lot, I ask him where he wants to go for lunch.

"I've got a hankering for a White Castle," he says. I know that he must miss his fast food routine, and it dawns on me how this type of 'comfort food' really does live up to its reputation for him.

"Then White Castle it is," I say. Splurging on Dear Old Dad.

The local White Castle joint is just down the street from Ellingwood, in a kind of a fast-food wonderland mini-mall.

I help Dad into the front seat of the car. I fold up the walker and slide it in behind the passenger seat.

As I plop into the driver's side, he looks around the car. I'm borrowing his Ford Taurus.

Normal routine over the years would have been for me to explicitly ask for permission to use his car, and I can feel him registering this slight flouting of the rules. Kind of a silent scolding I have become familiar with over the years. But then he exhales and lets it go. He realizes the rules have changed. "How's the car holding up?" he asks.

"Fine, fine," I say. "I've given it a nickname." I too want to change the rules.

"Oh, yeah? What?"

"The Raging Bull. Get it? Bull, it's a Taurus. And you sometimes had road rage in it, so I thought of it as kind of a tribute…"

He sighs. Corny joke. Not quite enough energy for a full laugh. And he surely must have heard the past tense "had road rage" rather than the present tense "have road rage," which rubs in the reality that he's not likely to be driving again.

I know he must be longing to drive again, longing for the feel of the leather steering wheel, probably like a retired cowboy yearns to saddle up one last time.

"Do you ever feel like driving again?" I ask, but I'm sincerely hoping he won't be tempted to ask me to let him get behind the wheel.

"Ah." He exhales deeply. "Nah, don't miss it. But it was good while it lasted."

I'm relieved.

"It's over now. No regrets."

This is a new attitude. Rewriting the rules!

I can tell he's in no mood for an extended outing, as he was just a few short months ago, but I was hoping for a longer car ride with Dad than just a quick trip to the local fast-food joint.

Our conversations in the car have always been the best way — maybe the *only* way — for me to bond with Dad, and I was hoping for a personal story or two to develop.

"Want to take a ride somewhere before lunch?" I ask, as we sit at the traffic light in front of Ellingwood.

Maybe he's reading my mind. "How about back to the house?" he suggests.

"Sure." I turn on my left turn signal and head out north.

We drive down Harrison Avenue and turn into Dad's neighborhood on Mitchell Drive. Left from Mitchell onto Ludlow Place. I pull into his driveway and turn off the ignition.

It feels very quiet inside the car. Deep inhale. "Want to go in?" I ask.

"Is anybody living there?" he asks, a bit confused.

"Well, *I'm* staying there now," I tell him. "Having wild parties every night. It's a great party house."

He smiles. Then gives a subtle shake of his head side to side.

"You sure?" I ask again.

"Yeah," he says. "It's OK. I don't want to stir things up. I know I'm not coming back here."

This is new territory. We sit a few moments longer.

I am almost ready to tease him with: "Hey, Dad. The office table is waiting for you if you want to go in to visit it."

"Are you sure? Sure, sure you don't want to go in?"

He has now forgotten about the office table and the potential mess that might await him. In reality, Kate dives into the pile of correspondence once a week or so, and though she never had Dad's flair for document juggling, she's extremely competent at getting things done. And similarly, though she would never name what Dad called "horseshit sifting," she can readily tell when a piece of correspondence is innocuous or bogus, and just throw it out rather than letting it fester on the desktop.

"Yeah, I just wanted to see the place. We can leave now." I detect a knot in his throat, reminding me of the time we visited the Greenview Café for the last time.

"Ready for lunch then?" I ask.

"Yep," he says, biting his lower lip. I start the car again, back out.

We drive a few minutes and park the Taurus near the front of the white building with the castle-like facade. The order comes quickly.

Dad wolfs down three or four of the tiny burgers, gobbling up a full order of fries and slurping a Diet Coke. *Where does he get this appetite?*

When we arrive back at Ellingwood, I look for the parking space close to the door, as Dad would do. Dad points out the one that's closer than the one I had spotted, half-hidden behind a gray van.

I pull in and turn off the ignition.

I can feel that some announcement is coming. I push the visor up and lean back, waiting for it.

"You can sell it," Dad announces. "The car, the house. Everything."

I look over at him, trying to absorb this. If anything represented Dad in his 'provider phase,' that is, in his entire adult life, it would be his house and his car. And now, "Sell it?"

"I'm sure you need the money to pay for all this sh…" He does a little whoopee circle with his right index finger, referring to the Ellingwood grounds. I'm sure he's going to say "shit," but he continues, "all this *stuff.*"

"You sure?" I ask, trying to soothe his agitation. "There's no rush to do this."

"Yeah. It's *time*," Dad says authoritatively.

I pause, waiting for his follow-up.

"Just be sure you get the best price for everything," he adds.

"Okay," I assure him.

I help Dad out of the car, remove his walker from the back seat, and get him positioned in the middle of his walker. We inch our way back to the front of Ellingwood. I realize he has slowed down considerably. Every step is a sort of walking meditation: roll walker forward, pause, breathe, step forward to meet it, pause, breathe. I know he will soon be using a wheelchair full-time. His legs, his spine, his heart, his lungs, all worn out, all reaching their expiration dates. Dad hasn't been floating these past eighty-some years.

We make our way toward the stately entry way, past the tiered Charlotte fountain, past the three aluminum flagpoles, past the powder-blue *Ellingwood Retirement Community* sign written invitingly in a storybook font. We finally make our way through the sliding glass doors and pause for a rest.

"You okay, Dad?" I ask. He's winded. He doesn't look up, but he nods, and moves the walker forward.

We pass the reception desk, and I exchange hello glances with Howard, who looks up from his computer screen. We trundle through the atrium and make our way down the hall to Room 103. We sidle into the room, undetected by Mom. She's sitting up in bed, staring out the window.

"You don't have to tell her about this," Dad whispers. He does the whirling motion with his finger to recall the conversation we had in the car.

I nod, giving him the steepled-fingers 'promise' gesture. "Yeah. Just between you and me."

I guide Dad to his bed, help him sit, then fold up the walker and move it aside. "That was a great lunch, Dad," I say, louder than necessary, in case Mom is registering any of this conversation. "You get some rest now, all right. I'll be back around dinner time."

Dad grunts, not at all in awe of my thespian performance, dragging his feet across the bed and plopping backwards on the bed. His eyes close and he is lightly snoring before I even stand up.

I glance over at Mom and see that she too has now leaned backward onto her pillow and is dozing.

I exit the room and walk down past the nurses' station. I give a thumbs up to Doris, the nutritionist, that today's lunch was a success — though I'm hoping she won't ask for details. I drop off Dad's walker behind the desk. Howard, the head nurse, has recently asked me to keep the walker here so that Dad doesn't try to get up and walk on his own. He's not quite as sure-footed as he used to be, but goddamn it, he *was*. There was a time when he really, really was light on his feet, nimble as a cat.

28. The Transition

I hear of people who have witnessed the decline of an elder talk about "the ideal departure." They say that the best way to go out is to have a full, vigorous life up until the end, and then, in the final few months or weeks, "take a dive," let it all go, and exit with dignity.

I don't know if anyone has ever actually seen a real person's demise go exactly like this, but the swan dive — a brief and graceful entry into the afterlife — seems like the perfect way to go. I saw Richard Drew's photograph of "The Falling Man" jumping out of the burning World Trade Center building on 9/11, quietly entering his inevitable death, in a manner of his own choosing. It seemed to me very elegant.

Dad would come close to this ideal of The Falling Man.

Shortly after our visit to White Castle, shortly after Kate arranged to sell Dad's car and the house, Dad took his plunge.

At one point, he transitioned to the wheelchair full-time. "No more four-four forties in these legs," he said, referring to his best time in the forty-yard dash. Nicknamed "Rip" for his blazing foot speed (something I did not inherit), Dad's athletic career at Roger Bacon High School would always be part of his legacy. (He still kept his letter jacket in the basement closet.)

From the transition to the wheelchair, it was just a matter of a few weeks before he began seriously wheezing. We had all thought his lungs would be the first body part to go.

Dad eventually lost interest in watching television, at one point placing the remote on his side table face down, the last game show consumed to the final Jeopardy question: "This American diver received a perfect ten score at the 1984 Olympics."

The saddest part of the transition may have been the final retiring of his crossword pen.

No more crossword puzzles to solve. Disconnected from a need to describe the world. Lexicon unplugged.

Isn't there an accolade for this? And the Cruciverbalist Lifetime Achievement award goes to…

Near the end, Dad was resting with his eyes closed for most of the day, still seated upright in his blue La-Z-Boy chair. He could be moved with help from an aide to his wheelchair when he needed to go the bathroom or to the dining hall, but he preferred the La-Z-Boy the rest of the time.

I am visiting, for the last time, it turns out, in late September. This is my sixth visit since Mom was diagnosed with Alzheimer's two plus years earlier.

The summer heat had now dissipated. The leaves on the sugar maples, the satin sycamores, the white ash are beginning to turn to buttery yellow, fiery orange and burgundy red.

I'm sitting next to Dad, leafing through the sports page of *the Cincinnati Enquirer.* "The Reds still have a shot this year," I announce, trying to inject some nostalgic cheer into the room.

I notice Dad stirring, but he remains quiet. I now feel the irrelevance, the irreverence of my baseball chatter. Dad is not planning to attend any more games.

"Mmmh. Is anyone here?" Dad is saying softly. "I want to open my eyes. But I can't."

What is Dad seeing? *My eyes are deep inside me, in another universe, on another plane. It's so empty in here, no shapes, no shadows. No color. Just reflections of light, changing hues.*

Dad's voice comes through, "Come here, come here." I feel him beckoning to me. He needs to say something.

"What is it, Dad?" I put my hand on his forehead and push back the wisps of gray hair.

Time has slowed down. There is no hurry for a response.

"I need…" he eventually says. I move closer to his lips. "*To know,*" he continues.

"Know… I need to know…," I repeat.

"*Zer,*" he says. I can tell this is getting difficult for him.

"Zer?" I echo back.

"An sing," he continues. *"Zer an sing els... do?"* he manages to string together these several syllables.

I'm starting to piece this together: "Is there *an sing*…anything?"

"Zer anysing els nee do?" he repeats, mustering all of his energy.

"Is there anything else you need to do?" I repeat slowly.

He's quiet. He's breathing deeply. I think I understand.

"No, Dad, nothing else you need to do. You've taken care of everything."

He seems to nod. He exhales intensely. *"Zat's goo,"* he utters at maximum volume. *Hhhhhhhh-huuuuuuuuu.*

His breathing is more labored than I have ever heard from him. "Can I… lie down now…?"

I call Kate over. She's been talking with Mom on the other side of the room.

We help Dad from his blue suede La-Z-Boy chair to his bed. "Here we go. One-two-three. Up you go." *Rmmphh.*

Mom is watching this dance intently, as we carefully choreograph Dad from his chair to his bed.

Maybe it's clear to her also: He will never be coming back to his chair.

She looks warmly at the scene, intently watching the man whom she often doesn't even recognize, but still knows he's very important to her. Watching him maintain his dignity as he struggles one last time to coax his body out of his chair and into his bed, his final place of rest.

"There you go, Dad. You can rest now," I say, stroking the top of his head, feeling the warmth of his body.

Once Dad is in his bed, we experience a deep exhale. All tension seems to dissolve from his body.

He was at peace. We covered him. Kate pats him on the chest, "You're okay, now. You just rest."

A moment of solitude.

But just then, Louise, one of the veteran nurses, comes cruising into the room, with her 'This is my wing and you play by my rules' attitude. "Now Daniel, why are you in your bed?" she clucks. "You know, I want you to stay in your chair until dinner time."

We wave her off. "It's okay. He wanted to lie down," we tell her.

"Well, you should have called me to come help you move him. I don't want him fallin' on the floor. Not on my watch. Unh-hunh."

But then the world stops for Louise also. She sees what has just transpired. Louise switches from officious administrator to gentle caretaker mode. She sits on the bed next to Dad and places a hand on his chest.

"You'll feel more relaxed here, Mr. Daniel," she says softly.

I feel as if we should console Dad's La-Z-Boy chair, sitting there beside him, all alone, like a loyal puppy waiting for him to come back, but knowing that they may have just said their final farewell.

No more scanning the horizon. No more rules. No more words. No more connections needed.

196

29. The Vigil

I've recently started fasting one day a week, not the whole day usually, maybe eighteen hours, from dinner on Saturday to noon on Sunday. It's not for any religious reason or health reason, really, but just to experience the sensation of craving and noticing how it eventually passes without being acted upon. That it's okay to feel hungry and not do something immediately to alter or quell that feeling. After a while, it leads to an altered state having nothing at all to do with hunger, and time passes differently. You're not looking forward to anything in particular, you've stopped planning your next action, you've stopped thinking about the need to satisfy.

Maybe this is how Dad is feeling now? He's on the sixth day of his 'hunger strike.' Dad is now dozing most of the time, awakening occasionally to open his eyes halfway and survey his surroundings. He is refusing food and water, but the hospice nurse will pop in the room regularly to wet his lips to protect him from complete dehydration.

Kate would sit by him as well, watching him breathe.

Knock, knock.

The nurse pops into the room, holding a paper Starbucks cup, and plops into the chair. Kate is seated on the bed, by Dad's feet.

"Hi, hon. How's Daniel today? Holding on, eh?"

She reaches over and strokes his legs, covered by his blanket. "Let me get Lester in here to change the sheets." She presses a few buttons on her phone and turns back to Dad. "Hi there, Daniel. How you doin'?" She looks into his closed eyes and squeezes his hand. "You want something to eat, honey? Daniel, you want something to eat?"

She knows the answer, but it's her job to ask. Dad is shutting down. Deliberately. Systematically. This is the ultimate project for the systems analyst: how to shut down one's life. It will end — the physical plane will end — and *he* will be the one to end it — when all of the systems completely cease to function. When he decides.

Lester, a tall athletic man about thirty years old, appears at the door, holding some sheets under his left arm.

"Daniel, honey, Lester here is going to change your sheets. Is that okay, sweetie?"

Lester moves over to the side of the bed and pats Dad's chest with his free hand. Lester had always been one of Dad's favorite aides, and they are about to share one last handclasp, one last dance.

"Hi there, Daniel. This'll just take a second," Lester says affectionately.

And then, in a well-practiced sleight of hand motion, Lester pulls off the top sheet with cupped fingertips, rolls it into a ball and floats it toward the door. Then he scoops Dad up with one hand, like a rag doll, and quickly pulls off the bottom sheet. Still cradling Dad in one arm, he masterfully replaces the sheet with a clean one in a matter of seconds. He places Dad gently down on the bed and covers him with a clean top sheet.

"There you go, mon. Good as new. See you later, Daniel," Lester chirps as he scoops up the used sheets and heads into the hall.

Well, maybe yes, maybe no.

Another cursory knock at the door.

"Hi, I'm Doctor Alvarez. How's he doing?" The doctor picks up Dad's right wrist, flopping loosely like a rag doll.

Kate turns to him a questioning look. "He seems sleepy all the time. Is this because of some medication?"

"He's not taking any medication," the doctor says. "This is just a natural process."

It sounds as if the doctor is about to give a philosophical lesson about what this passage is like.

He continues, "Yup, this is what dying looks like."

That's it!?

He then adds, "But I have no idea why it's taking so long."

Well, some of us *do* know why. It's never been a good idea to try to interfere with a 'systems guy.' Dad is now in the final process of releasing from his body — and you can be sure he'll do this in his own way, on his own schedule, not on the punch-in punch-out timetable of the hospice staff. He will linger over some unsettled issue or some uncompleted relationship — like he always has — until it's resolved. And most likely he doesn't want anyone to be present when he decides to check out.

I imagine Dad is in his own world now, earthly time disconnected, cravings all subsided, game clock off, reliving defining moments, re-dreaming both fulfilled and unfulfilled dreams.

Maybe he's remembering his childhood, growing up above the Greenview Café, in a crowded apartment with his three sisters. And maybe he's remembering how his youngest sister Maddie got sick with pneumonia, how she just wouldn't get better. And the hushed gasping tones between his mother and father and the doctor.

Maybe Dad is dreaming of his days in the army, the "rotten luck" of being captured, imprisoned, humiliated. Wondering if this is how life will end, incarcerated and starving. Will I ever see her again? My fiancée, the woman in red, waiting in Cincinnati, the mystical city of seven hills? Will she know that I tried to make it back for her? That I really *intended* to come back for her?

Maybe he's dreaming of visiting Dresden with me, long after the war was over, setting foot for the first time on the land of his great-grandfather. Gawking at the rubble still piled up near the busy streets decades later, the ever-present aftermath of a horrific attack, imagining his own distant cousins desperately pulling at chunks of steaming concrete looking for their loved ones.

Maybe he's dreaming of his visit with me to the Hiroshima War Memorial, again many years after the reckoning of the end of this godawful war. Though I was always the one trying to pry into his memories of war, it was Dad who asked me to take him to Hiroshima while I was living in Japan. I remember his hands resting on the glass cases, adrift in his own thoughts, surveying the scarred items of children, incinerated lunch boxes, tattered backpacks, frozen instantaneously at the moment of death.

"How was that for you?" I ask him as we exit the memorial, trying to snap him out of his reverie.

"How can they ever forgive us?" he whispers, gazing outward at the horizon.

Or maybe he's moved on past the war. Maybe he's dreaming of strolling down the boardwalk at Coney Island on the banks of the Ohio River with Emma Hofmann, his new girlfriend with the Rita Hayworth flowing hair, and thinking, *Yes, yes, she's the one.*

The most poetic thing I had ever heard from Dad was once when I asked him how he fell in love. "I don't have the words to describe how I know this, but I felt like I was feeling something *spiritual* for the first time. There was something in the air between us," he had said.

Maybe he's dreaming of baseball, the timeless beauty of coordinated motion. The crack of the bat, the roar of the crowd.

Or maybe he's dreaming of all these things at once, in a wonderful fusion of timelessness.

202

30. *The Promise*

Dad is near the end of the seventh day of his voluntary 'hunger strike,' only having taken a few sips of water all week.

As the end of the day shift rolls around on Friday, the hospice nurse attending Dad has decided that it's over. Or at least she's had enough. "Sorry, this is all I'm contracted for. I'll have to get clearance from the front office for an extension," the nurse says to Kate, as she packs her things. "I'm off at five today and that's all we're contracted for. I'll check with the office on Monday morning."

She glances at her watch. It's already a bit past five. She packs up, turns and leaves, as if the shift buzzer on the factory floor on the auto assembly plant has just sounded, the conveyor belt has come to a skidding stop, and she's stepping back from her riveter, throwing her work gloves on her workstation table, and walking toward the locker room. *See y'all on Monday!*

Success! Dad has finally outlasted the hospice crew. The seven-day hospice contract has expired. That's the maximum, you can't extend it. Dad is not supposed to last this long without food and water, so guess what, you're on your own now.

I'm alone at last. Now I can do this the right way.

"Have a great weekend," she bids everyone on her way out.

Kate stares in disbelief as the nurse scurries out of the room. She's fuming, but as with so many events in the past couple of years, there is no precedent, no set of guidelines for how you're supposed to react.

Mom takes this bit of commotion in stride. One of the benefits of late-stage dementia is that you only see 'the big picture.' That's all there is. She's reached the place Buddhists call समाधी — "sa-ma-dhi," a state of meditative union. Little *bip-bip-bips* on the radar screen don't register. The comings and goings of the individual players in the human drama have no effect on her consciousness.

Mom is simply resting in her wheelchair, knowing by her body clock that it's about five p.m., awaiting someone to push her to the dining room. After several days observing Dad in his comatose state, she has become accustomed to his still, lightly-breathing body in the bed on the other side of the room. He's creating a soft *whoo-whoo* sound, rhythmically vibrating in the room, comforting her with the steady passage of time. She's barely been fazed by the rotating shift of nurses who stay with him, wetting his lips with a moist cloth, giving him a sponge bath, gently lifting his frail body to change sheets.

Because it is now dinner time, Kate moves toward Mom to take her to the cafeteria. But first a few adjustments. A change of sweaters — "It's getting a bit chilly." A bit of makeup — "This new shade of red looks really good on you." Brushing her silver hair — "Oh, I love how shiny your hair is after your shampoo."

Kate also feels the contrast between preparing the details of her mother's appearance — Mom's well-being really — and witnessing her father's physicality melt away from his body. Mom, too, has adjusted to the perfunctory departure of the hospice nurse, but through a very different mental process. In any event, it's not important now, have to attend to matters at hand. But Kate makes a mental note: she will be certain to "have a word" with the appropriate administrator on Monday morning. She'll set things right.

As Kate wheels Mom's chair past Dad's bed, she notices a slight shift in his breathing pattern. A kind of clutching and shortness in the pulsation pattern. Kate leaves Mom at the foot of the bed, goes up to Dad, kisses him on the forehead. She turns to go, then pauses and turns back to him and whispers in his ear, "It's okay, Dad. She'll be fine. I promise. We're going to dinner now. We'll be back."

Mom overhears this, and though during this entire week of hospice, she hasn't spoken directly to Dad, she pats him on his foot, covered with a gold sock, that is dangling out from under the sheet. She mouths her version of what Kate has just said, "It's okay. I'll be back. I promise."

And then Kate pushes Mom toward the cafeteria, to join her newest table mates. Sarah has recently passed away, and Fred is in an intensive care unit. Now a woman named Brenda sits on her left and a man named Hector is seated on her right.

Mom feasts on some brownish-gray nebulous meatloaf, a mound of mushy peas, a slice of cherry cobbler, her customary never-on-time milk, and a cup of decaf coffee, a little on the too-cool side.

Kate sits with Mom, chatting and joking with the staff. At first, she wants to share the nurse abandonment story with them, but then she realizes, *Nah, it'll just come off as an attack. We're all in this together.* An important principle of successful communication: the perlocutionary effect of an utterance, its consequential impact on the listener, is just as important as the illocutionary force, the intent of the speaker.

When Kate leaves the dining hall, less than an hour later, she passes the nurses' station. No Howard.

"Anything wrong?" Kate asks Loreen, the aide at the desk. Loreen swallows hard and points down the hall, toward Room 103, Mom and Dad's room.

On instinct, Kate decides to leave Mom in her wheelchair at the nursing station. "I'll be right back," she assures Mom. Mom is accustomed to these random acts of abandonment, but is calm, knowing that her caretakers always do keep their word.

Entering Room 103, Kate sees Howard standing next to Dad's bed, holding Dad's limp hand. "Oh, Kate," Howard says, "I'm so sorry. He's gone."

Kate lays her hand on Dad's chest, and though his body is in the same position as an hour before, it is clear that Dad has departed. His torso is waxy and hollow. His face is serene, all struggle departed from his body, no further intentions to communicate.

And so we all let go. The paradoxical question that we have climbed to mountaintops to seek answers to now becomes clear. *No, you don't need to suffer when you die. Yes, you do need to understand the nature of suffering before you can let go.*

31. *The Day After*

I am in a large, deserted building, still under construction. It feels like a Depression-era New York high-rise, and I'm wearing tattered construction clothes and beat-up work boots. I'm walking on a network of massive steel girders, looming high above the ground, needing to get to the other side. I am precariously balancing to keep from plunging to a certain death in the morass of jagged structures below me. I feel almost destined to fall, but I keep edging forward, one step, one step.

I look down for some guidance, though I know I will feel dizzy and disoriented. I see the earth below is uneven, pitching up and down in small patches, spotted with ponds in a rainbow of colors. At the very center of these ponds is an open pool of swirling white pearl- like liquid. As I look closer, I can see vague shapes, but they keep moving and changing form, so I can't identify what they are. Then I hear something. The liquid is inviting me to do something. It asks me something and I pause. Sorry, I don't understand, I say. Yes, you do, the liquid answers. Don't pretend that you don't understand.

I ask what I have done to deserve this, and it answers calmly, that it is simply "my time." Then I feel a deep wave of relief, from the top of my head down to my toes. The tension is gone, magically, completely. As I look down again, I notice the beams are rusting and growing thinner and thinner. I understand now what is being asked of me. For a moment I feel a slight resistance, a clinging. But then as my fingers rise to touch my forehead softly in a sign of obedience, this feeling of hesitation subsides. My skin, starting with the top of my head, peels off smoothly, as if it had been awaiting this release for some time. Invited by the white glowing pool, cool and inviting yet bubbling quite actively below me, I let it all go.

I am at once absorbed, consumed, accepted as part of this luxurious pearl-like liquid.

The meaning of the dream seems clear to me.

***

Squeak-squeak-squeeeeeeak.

An aide, Leonard, is wheeling Dad's empty bed out of the room.

Mom sits upright in her wheelchair and takes notice. *What are you doing?* her look asks.

"Hi, Mrs. Bron, just taking this over to 209. Sorry to bother you." He smiles and goes about his business.

"Where is that man who lives here?" she asks in protest. "That's *his* bed."

Kate and I are seated next to Mom. "Yes, that's Dad's bed," Kate says calmly, referring to the portable bed that Leonard is about to trundle away.

Leonard turns to me before he exits the room. He mouths quietly, "Sorry for your loss, Gabri-el," he says, stressing the last syllable in his lilting Jamaican accent. And then he adds, "DanYEL DAT he ma BRADdah," nodding to the empty bed. *Daniel was my brother.* He sniffles deeply, wipes his eye, and smiles loyally, biting his lower lip, as he departs.

"Where is he? Is he still asleep?" she asks, associating the bed, now vacated from the room, with sleep.

"You know, he was really sick," Kate begins, knowing she must connect with Mom on the right level of explanation.

I look at Mom's eyes as she begins to calculate what Kate is telling her.

"And sometimes sick people die."

I think Kate has rehearsed this account. I know that she has been fretting over how to explain the situation to Mom. Kate, more than anyone in Mom's world, knows how deeply this will affect her.

Mom seems to accept this. It's a perfect explanation. I might have said it differently, leaving out the sickness part, since I didn't think of Dad as being sick at the end. Actually, I *never* thought of him as being sick at any time in his entire life.

Then I realized Kate is using a code that Mom will understand best. She looks up at Kate. "Oh, he died?"

Kate hasn't wanted to hear her say this word, hoping that there was a way to apprehend without bringing up death.

"Yes, Mom, he died," Kate says, gripping her right hand.

Mom nods gravely, her head going up and down several times, slowly. She understands this. She understands this better than any of us. In her own fused way of thinking now, she most certainly is absorbing all of this, in ways that we cannot detect.

And now, looking at her, I feel a sense of gratitude as well. Gratitude coming from her. Mom is grateful that she is being told this directly, without softening, without coding, without taking her own fragility into account.

Then, in a moment that seems to last forever, I see a look of profound sadness drawing across her face, from her forehead, down through her chin. A recognition that a life, an entire life, a mutual life that she had built with this person is now gone. And the realization that she wasn't there to witness the end.

There is nothing more for Kate or me to say.

"I wish I had a chance to say goodbye," Mom says, gazing intently at the space where Dad's bed had been. "He was a good man."

Sehnsucht. Beyond words. The world is too full. The disease had not robbed her of her innate yearning, the meaning of being human.

Kate decides to use Mom's most native language. "Let's say a prayer for him."

And she stoops down in front of Mom's wheelchair and holds both of Mom's hands, supported by the arms of her wheelchair.

They recite together, in a rising crescendo: "Our father, who art in heaven, hallowed be Thy name, Thy kingdom come, Thy will be done…"

Mom's voice is loud and clean again, lofting upward. She is teaching all of us the correct words, the exact vibration to use to understand this.

And now I hear her voice, stretching back through time, the same resonance, timbre, fluidity, envelope, the same sustain and decay. The same voice she had when she used to sing *Que Sera, Sera* to me as a child, the same quiet voice she had when she murmured incantations quietly in her prayer room, the same soothing voice she used in her affirmations with me in the emergency room as a child, "You'll be all right, you'll be all right." I can hear them all simultaneously, a miraculous quality of the harmonics of sound. She is strong and vibrant, and she is leaving the imprint of her voice on the world.

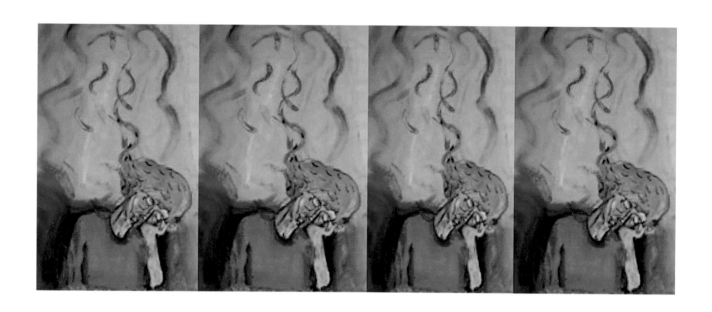

32. Winter Jasmines

Because I know tomorrow his faithful gelding heart will be broken
when the spotted mare is trailered and driven away,
I come today to take him for a gallop on Diaz Ridge.
Returning, he will whinny for his love.
Ancient, spavined, her white parts red with hill-dust,
her red parts whitened with the same, she never answers.

There are days when you wake up and you know today is a day when your heart is about to be broken. You know that something transitional is going to happen. You know that whatever it is, it's going to be more powerful than your ability to control it, so like a bronco rider, you hope that you can stay upright for the requisite eight seconds, to be present when the message is delivered. And if you do, you will be proud.

I'm sitting at the breakfast table at Ellingwood with Mom.

Slrrrrp.

Mom takes a loud last sip of her decaf coffee, indicating that it's time to go. A slight grimace as she curls her tongue around the inside of her mouth. "It's a little too cold," she chides, directed at whomever is listening. She had always liked her coffee a certain temperature. Quality didn't matter, but temperature certainly did.

As I wheel Mom away from the dining room, I suggest a little side trip. "How about a walk in the garden?" I suggest.

"I can't walk," she says.

Ah, I didn't need to use the word *walk* either!

"No, I know that," I say. "I mean, I'll push you through the garden. A last dance! How about that?"

She's quiet. We speak now in a language of pauses, and I weigh this one to mean that she acquiesces. I hold open the cafeteria doors, push her up and along the wheelchair ramp and into the garden.

I pause at the first fork in the path. "You know what I love about gardens?" I say.

No response, but I continue anyway. "I love how everything continues somehow, some things die and some things come to seed and they keep flowering."

"Oh," she acknowledges. I am simply voicing lessons she has given to me and countless others over the years. At this moment, she has probably forgotten that she is the one who taught me to look closely at things in nature, to see the details, to understand how beauty is always disarming, always surprising. I want to engage her, for what I sense may be the last time in a lesson about flowers, but she's definitely not picking up on this. Now, she is just tired. No more lessons to teach, and she doesn't want to hear her student rambling on about what he's learned. Yawn.

We move softly along the path; she looks down from time to time and tilts her head to one side, indicating that I should stop. She inspects the flowers that still bloom in winter: the yellow leather leaf mahonias, the fragrant purple daphnes, the waxy pink-and-white Christmas roses.

And ah, yes, the golden winter jasmines, the flowers that hang on to their bloom so much longer than you would expect. She knows them all by their biological names, their true names, their true essence, though she can't conjure up the words just now.

After only a half-circle around the garden, she cranes her head back toward me. "I'd like to go in now. I'm too tired. I just want to take a nap," she says. "I'm a little worn out today."

"Nothing wrong with that," I say. "Let's just rest."

Since Dad died, Mom has become noticeably quieter, more pensive. I take her back to her room. I help Mom off with her shoes — her ankles are quite swollen — and shimmy her up out of her chair and into her bed. She adjusts herself along the length of the bed and quickly pulls her red cotton cover over her, up to her chin. She's cold.

Mom's looking up toward the ceiling. She has tears in her eyes. "I don't want you to take this the wrong way…" she says. I think of some possible continuations. "But you make me cry."

"In a good way?" I query.

"Oh, you," she says, smiling a bit through her sobbing. "In a good way, yes. I don't know. It's just that you make me remember all the things I used to do."

I can't resist reciprocating. "Well, Mom, you know, you make me cry too sometimes."

"I do?" she asks, surprised.

"Yes, you make me think about all the things you've taught me. All the things you've done for me."

She looks up through her tearing eyes, the twinkle being drowned out. "Oh, now you're getting me all sentimental."

"Well, you've done so much." I realize her tears are not about doing or not doing, have nothing to do with achieving or not achieving, having taught anything, having given anything. These tears are more about understanding, about understanding that at some point there will be nothing left to do, nothing else to say.

She's sobbing now.

"You've done all you can do," I say as I rub her left forearm that's over the top of the red cover. I see a little sigh of relief. She knows I'm not going to ask any more questions, not do any more interpreting. She clutches my forearm in an impossible Escher-like pose.

"It's okay to let go, Mom." I'm not sure if I mean let go of my arm, or let go of the effort to do more, or just let go of everything. I am leaving, you are staying; you are leaving, I am left behind. A chiasmus dance.

She lets go of my arm and her hand trickles down slowly to rest beside mine. In seconds, she's drifting off to sleep, much more painlessly than I've ever seen her do. I detect a smile, though it is more like a complete absence of holding on, which I feel is the same thing.

33. Silver Stockings

In the murky water are several grayish-blue octopus-like creatures. Despite the cloudiness, I can see them clearly, each detail of their spongy bodies. Each has a uniquely-shaped squishy head, multiple bulging eyes the size of grapefruits glaring into the deep, warmish water. Each of these creatures is patterned in its own unique patches of emerald and turquoise, speckled with rose, gold, white, magenta.

They swim quietly — amazingly without any sound — slowly, timelessly in mysterious circular patterns, all coordinated, though it is not clear to me that they even notice each other.

Then I see it! Ah, they do recognize the others. Each one subtly acknowledges the company of the other swimmers with a gentle connection through the eyes. Beyond this silent connection, it is clear to me they are all seeking something.

Then, suddenly, unannounced, the warm waters above me, part. At this moment, I realize that I too am an octopus, like they are. But I feel I am the smallest of these creatures, and paralyzed in my position, not swimming freely like the others. I feel an enormous swirling motion, much greater than any force I had ever experienced. Then I am caressed and eased upward by a spongy arm. I am safe. I know there is nothing else I need to do.

It places me on its large lap, embraced within its own tentacles. I breathe deeply as my small body comes to life, now playing with the larger one holding me. The larger one focuses its many eyes on me, drawing all of my eyes simultaneously towards it.

I now become beautiful, a glowing topaz blue, shining outward. I begin to smile and play, being fondled and protected by the larger being.

I look up for the first time at the large one beside me. It appears to look the same as me, glowing bright blue, though every limb is bigger, every feature bolder, more dignified. The larger one, with its gooey arms, slick with slime, is now focused solely on my mirrored beauty.

I'm groggy as I relive the previous night's dream. I seem to be having vivid dreams virtually every night recently.

Parking my car in a vacant space near the door, I stumble my way to Room 103 at Ellingwood, where my sister Kate is waiting for me. As I enter the room, I see that she is already occupied with Mom.

Kate is sitting with her, at her bedside. "He came for me last night," Mom tells Kate. I hear this pronouncement clearly, the most vibrant voice I've heard from Mom in months.

"What do you mean? Who came for you?" Kate asks.

"Your father. He came to… g-g-get me," she says, searching for the word. "But I wasn't ready," she adds.

"He came to *meet* you? Maybe it was a dream," Kate offers, grabbing her hand.

Mom hasn't quite been herself these past several weeks since Dad died. Of course, she hasn't actually "been herself"— the engaged, gregarious, life-of-the-party presence that everyone knew — for some time now, not really since Bridge Night, when she suddenly forgot the rules of her favorite card game. The decline, the displacement, all since then had taken its toll, and now being alone without the tacit love of her lifelong partner.

But this is not a normal exchange with Mom, helping her to reconstruct missing bits from her memory. The tone of this conversation has a transformational quality to it.

Since Dad died, she would ask every day if "that man" was coming back. She would still look behind the curtain, over at the bed on the other side of the room, where Dad used to sleep. She would anxiously gaze into the place he used to be, poised to ask him something. He had always been the one to answer questions, to fix things, to rescue her.

"He came to me to take me away, but I told him I wasn't ready."

Kate now begins to take in what she is saying. "You weren't ready?"

"No, I didn't have my sil, sli, silver stockings."

"Your *silver* stockings? You mean, your *silk* stockings?"

Mom used to tell the stories of growing up during the Depression with five sisters, three older and two younger. They all had to share everything. Sometimes one item for two of them. Mom and her sister Diana shared a bed for years, as well as clothes, books, toys. One tortoiseshell hairbrush, one Bakelite Supreme hair dryer.

And in addition to perpetual hand-me-downs — Mom claims she never wore anything new — the Hofmann sisters had shared a few items of expensive clothing, including one pair of silk stockings. They took turns, but if one of them had a very special occasion and could lobby hard enough, she might be able to 'have dibs' on the stockings.

"Yes, my silver stockings," Mom repeats. "Where are they? I can't find them. Who has them?" She looks around the room anxiously, wringing her hands.

Kate nods knowingly. "Well, I'll tell you what, Mom. *I'll* find your stockings for you. I bet that Diana has them. Yes, Diana probably has them." Mom nods, reassured that she has been understood. "Tell you what. I'll talk to her and get them for you."

Mom nods sympathetically. She can forgive Diana for this minor transgression. "Schwe prbmblmy hhd dmm." The left side of Mom's mouth is not moving properly as she tries to speak. "Yes, Mom, she probably hid them, but I'll get them back for you."

Diana had died many years earlier, the first of her siblings to pass away, but Mom still talked about her fondly from time to time, as if she dropped in for frequent visits.

Kate squeezes Mom's right hand knowingly. "Tell you what: The next time Dad comes, the next time you hear his voice, you tell him that you're ready. Tell him that you're wearing your silk stockings. Just tell him, he'll know. Tell him you're ready to go with him, okay?"

"Okay," Mom says, calming down. She's grateful for this solution to her dilemma. All of her life, her family, her religion has ingrained in her that one must hang on as long as humanly possible. That leaving voluntarily is not acceptable.

The final act is the hardest. You wonder if you have represented everything that has led up to this moment. You wonder if you have been true to your part. You wonder if it was worthwhile to fall in love, only to know that one day you must say goodbye. You wonder if you will ever be able to let go.

Up until that time, you feel that there is always some hope, some miracle waiting to pop, to transform everything into a jubilant parade.

Or in the case of this god-awful disease: a white-frocked savior running down the hall, right as your mother is expiring, holding up a test tube: *We found it, we found it. We've found the cure! Tell her to wait!*

No, that's not going to happen. There won't be a heroic Hollywood ending, a miraculous rescue from pain and suffering.

In the final act, you simply inhale and become, for a moment, a fresh-faced, twenty-five-year-old beauty queen again, in an emerald-and-turquoise dress, adorned with rose, gold, and magenta speckles, spinning gracefully on your peep-toe heels, smiling for the flashing cameras.

You realize the final act will be uninterrupted and intimate, without critics or censors, without costumes or scripts, without an audience. But it will be elegant you will be embraced in your own mirrored beauty.

34. Six White Horses

I wonder how many stories I have been part of that end sadly. There must be a lot of them. Or is it that so many stories — and all love stories — end in separation and loss? Or maybe it's that grief has its way of punctuating stories, of overwhelming them, of commandeering every event, hijacking every memory in its path.

One time, decades earlier, when I was home from university, Mom saw me in a reclined position on the couch, reading a book. She was sitting in her chair by the window, reading one of her Catholic mission magazines, I suppose. "Is that a book for school? What's it about?" she asked.

"Literature," I said somewhat dismissively. She seldom asked about my schoolwork, even back in high school. "World Literature. It's a class I'm taking for my major."

I remember that I loved my literature classes — the revelations, the unexpected tremors of emotions. It felt like a secret pleasure that I was able to indulge in. But I also dreaded the sheer amount of effort required to do all of the reading. And now, I was in somewhat of the familiar student panic mode: I didn't want to be disturbed, trying to reach my required quota of educational input before classes started up the following week.

"Oh, that's nice," Mom said, showing a bit of curiosity. Mom had never gone to college, an idea never entertained by her working-class family, her father a carpenter, her mother a stay-at-home parent taking care of nine children. Mom was forced to get a job right away after high school, at Seagram's bottling plant to help out her family.

"So how is the class?" she asked. This was new territory, maybe the first time she had ever asked so explicitly about my classes.

"Yeah, it's okay," I said. I put down the book. "Opens my eyes to stuff I wouldn't read on my own." I had learned to be somewhat guarded about expressing an interest in literature or art around Mom or her family, particularly her brothers, as it was often met with ridicule or at least a rolling of eyes. *How pretentious!* Most of my cousins, male and female, went directly into trades right after high school, and I often got the message that college-educated kids are "elitist."

She sensed my discomfort. "Well, good for you." I went back to my book.

"Can you read me something?" she asked, persisting. "Maybe it'll open my eyes too."

"All right," I said, randomly opening my brick-like book with its imaginative title *A Review of World Literature*. "How about this? It's a kind of poem. It's by Rumi. He was a Persian poet."

She nodded and winced a bit, calling me out for being a bit too pedantic. She has put down her magazine now. "What's it called?" she asked.

"The Guest House."

She leaned forward as I began to read.

This being human is a guest house. Every morning a new arrival. A joy, a depression, a meanness, some momentary awareness, comes as an unexpected visitor. Welcome and entertain them all.

I looked up from the book and noticed that she is smiling lightly at this image. Her eyes had drooped shut.

Even if they're a crowd of sorrows, who violently sweep your house empty of furniture, still treat each guest honorably. He may be clearing you out for some new delight.

I didn't actually know what this meant — welcoming theft, welcoming violence? Being passive when someone or something invades your life? 'Turning the other cheek'? I noticed that Mom still had her eyes closed, and was breathing slowly, somehow going deeper.

The dark thought, the shame, the malice, meet them at the door laughing and invite them in.

I looked up, a bit embarrassed that I had shared this with her. *Too much? I went too far?*

Mom took a final deep breath and began to wink her eyes open.

"Is that it?" she asked.

"Yeah, that's all of it. He just wrote these cryptic little…" I stopped myself, knowing that she didn't need an explanation.

"What do *you* think it means?" I asked her.

222

"Oh, I suppose it means that you never know what is coming your way." She pauses and shrugs. "But you have to take it all in. Sometimes it's hard to recognize a blessing."

***

One night in February, Mom had a stroke.

The following morning, she was unable to move the left side of her body. Howard noticed this when he was making his rounds. The left side of her face didn't move when she said, *"Good morning." Gwwwd mwwwnggg.*

Howard calls Kate to tell her. "Kate, I think you need to get over here," he tells her calmly. "When I came in to check on your mother this morning, I could see that she had had a stroke during the night."

When Kate arrives, and sees Mom with Howard at her side, he asks right away, "Should we take her to the hospital? Maybe there's something they can do?" Howard knows that Mom has a DNR — "do not resuscitate" — order and he needs authorization from Kate for any medical action.

Kate has visions of insertions of balloons for thrombectomy procedures and injections of plasminogen activators.

"No," Kate answers, cutting him off kindly before he goes into detail. This is a difficult decision, but one she has been preparing to make. "This is her time."

Over the next few days, Mom is bedridden. She speaks very little, with the left side of her face and mouth not moving, what speech she does attempt is slurred. She takes some nourishment in her bed, slurping up bits of gelatin and sipping milk. She sleeps more, enclosing herself snugly into her bedding, pulling the sheets up to her eyeballs. Each day, she slips away just a bit more, diving just a bit deeper, nodding peacefully as she sleeps.

Kate stays with her, arranging to take more time off work. She's chatting to her, even though she doesn't respond, giving her daily news about family members, humming songs, massaging her arms. Sometimes just reading a book while Mom dozes.

On Friday, at the end of his workday, Howard comes in, walks over, and leans against the metal railing of Mom's bed. She's sleeping peacefully. He takes her right hand in both of his: "I'm leaving now, Emma. You're a real sweetheart. It's been wonderful to know you." He pats her folded hands and lays them back onto her stomach.

Kate says, "Well, Howard, you know, she may just be here when you get back to work on Monday morning." Always hopeful.

Howard smiles as he departs.

The next day, Kate can detect a further retreat by Mom. She calls in the priest for a final visit. "Father Leo" arrives within an hour, a stocky man with a graying beard, wearing his black frock and draped in a magnificent gold-embroidered epitrachelion. He quietly enters the room.

He gives a soft handshake and whispered greeting to Kate and then approaches Mom's bed. "Hello, Emma," he says in a friendly tone. He knows her well, as she regularly attends Sunday services at the Ellingwood chapel where he often says Mass.

Leaning against the rail of the bed, he deftly pulls out a small vile of golden oil from his pocket, squeezes a few drops on his fingertips.

Crouching toward Mom's body, barely moving with her breath, he dabs the healing oil on her wrists and intones the ritual words:

"Adjutórium nostrum in nómine Dómini." Our help is in the name…

Sh-sh-sh. Shu-shu-shu. "Per istam sanctam unctiónem." Through this intention… *Sh-sh-shu.* "May the Lord forgive you for what you have done." Sh-*shu-shu.* "May this be a sign of the glory that is to come." *Shu-shu-shu.* "Amen."

When he finishes, he removes the red-and-gold stole from around his neck, folds it carefully, places it under his arm, and leans in to Mom. "Emma, let's pray together," he says, beginning to recite the Lord's Prayer.

Mom, who has not spoken in days, begins to chime in, directly on cue, in the loud, animated voice of an eight-year-old child: "Our Father, who art in heaven…Thy kingdom come, thy will be done…" *Sh-sh-shu.*

Intoned articulately all the way to the end. Then she is silent again.

A Buddhist priest might have said it differently: *Lokah Samastag Sukhino Bhavantu.* May we all be free of suffering and the root of suffering. *Shu-shu-shu.*

***

Kate called me — along with each of my siblings individually — that night from Mom's bedside. Though I hadn't recalled my memory of sharing the Rumi poem with Mom in years, that's the poem I conjured up when I received her call: *Even if your visitor is a crowd of sorrows, who violently sweep your house empty of furniture, still treat each guest honorably. He may be clearing you out for some new delight.*

Kate didn't need to say much: "It seems like it's time."

I ask if I might be able to talk with Mom one last time. We both know by this time that communication is ruled by intent and connection, not by an exchange of messages. She says, "Sure" and puts me on speaker while holding the phone near Mom's ear. I start to remind Mom of the story of the Rumi poem, but realize it's too complicated, too remote. No more embeddings, no more recall tests. Instead, I ask her if I can sing her a song. Of course, she doesn't answer, but I continue.

"Here's a song that you used to sing to us when we were little."

I begin humming, not quite sure what will come out: *mmm-mmmm-mmm-mmmm-mmmm-mmmm.*

I then feel as if I'm channeling words from somewhere:

We'll all go out to meet her when she comes...

She'll be loaded with bright angels when she comes...

She will neither rock nor totter when she comes...

She will run so level and steady when she comes...

She will take us to the portals when she comes...

Oh, who will drive the chariot when she comes...

I don't know anything about the story of the lyrics — I didn't realize I even knew them! —but this feels like the right healing song for now. And it seems, for the moment, that Mom herself was a healer — certainly she resonated with so many of the early "Sorrow Songs" of the south and sang them to us. Like this one.

Kate leans in and picks up the phone. "You know, I think she hears you. Her eyes are moving."

Maybe she's searching for something, I wonder.

****

That night, at five in the morning, back in her own bed, Kate receives a call from the Ellingwood nurse on duty, Doreen.

"Kate, this is Ellingwood. I'm calling to tell you that it's over."

I imagine that Dad really did come for her that night, maybe driving a chariot. I imagine that he called her softly, called her by her name, maybe a special name that only he had for her.

I imagine that Mom was waiting for him, sitting steadily on her doorstep, silk stockings pulled up. She would have clarity, certainty that he would come this time, signaling to her the moment in a song, or in a poem, or in a magical code that they alone had created.

And I imagine that Mom moved toward him, in whatever form he appeared, now dancing, almost floating, holding onto Dad's arm as they found their way back home.

35. *Rasa Yatra*

I am standing at the top of a small rise, the spot my father had chosen for himself and my mother as a final resting place. A soft breeze sways the leaves of the sycamore trees above us — *ffffeeeewwwww* — overlooking the lake at Gate of Heaven cemetery. The burial grounds, an expanse of rolling hills, with a natural lake in the center, sits away from the bustle of Cornell Road, not far from where my mother and father lived the final chapter of their life together.

From this vista, the Gate of Heaven, on a clear day, you can see a long way. You can count them: one, two, three, four, five, six, seven. The Seven Hills of Cincinnati: Mount Adams, Fairmount, Auburn, Mount Echo, Mount Airy, Vine Street Hill, Mount Lookout. My mother once told me that *shin-shin-athi* was the expression for "upon seven peaks" in the language of the Shawnee, the original inhabitants of the area. She had a gift for languages, for understanding codes. My father had a different story. He told me the city was named by an organization of veteran Revolutionary War officers, in honor of a Roman hero, Lucius Quinctius Cincinnatus. He had a gift for historical references and testimonials.

Maybe both of their versions of the origin story are true. Or maybe they've fused into a different kind of truth.

The wind is whistling and I pull my coat up around my neck. I'm having trouble finding their graves, feeling like I am walking in circles. Though I was at both burials within the past year, one the previous December, one earlier this year in February, the setting seems foreign to me. The squishy terrain beneath me gives me the sensation of walking on the moon. I realize that when I was here for the funerals, I was always following a procession of people and rituals, not really paying attention to details — like exactly where the graves are located. So now, on my own, I feel lost.

As I often do when I'm trying to recall something, I go into a kind of inner mantra helping my brain reorganize. Aum… I continue wandering in the cemetery, repeating to myself: *Section 3, near a loping sycamore tree, on an upslope, overlooking the lake. Section 3, near a loping sycamore tree, on an upslope, overlooking the lake.* I'm hoping that the repetition of the cues will trigger the actual full-scale eidetic memory, but it's not working. All of the sections, all of the hills are looking identical to me, and indeed the lake is visible from virtually every vantage point. It crosses my mind that I may *never* find the graves.

Tempted to give up, I look down, rather than up. There they are — right in front of me. Seeing my parents' gravestones now, as if for the first time, I involuntarily crumple to my knees. I had not anticipated the effect this discovery would have on me.

As if observing myself from the trees above, I can see my back, leaning forward, inspecting the stones. Only now do I realize that I had set myself a purpose for this visit, a variation of one of Jake's Rules about preparation. I brought a roll of Brawny paper towels and a plastic spray bottle of Windex. I'm going to clean the gravestones.

Starting with Dad's stone on the right, I squirt the bottle deliberately on blackish-blue surface, multiple pulses, and the *pchit pchit pchit* sound seems to echo through the hills. Dedicated to my task now, I manuever my fingers inside the towels into the engraved letters spelling out their names. The black granite is such a noble stone, reminding me of the unfathomable depths of a star-filled night sky. But its surface is surprisingly delicate, accumulating dust and grit from the passing winds, particularly up here on the hill. But a few spritzes of this magical blue fluid and a bit of elbow grease wipes it all away. *Pchit pchit pchit.* Wipe, wipe, wipe.

At some point after he retired, Dad went through an intense period of family history archiving, detailing every fact and facet of our ancestry that he could discover. During that time, he thought it prudent to prepare for his own passing. Though Mom and we kids thought he was being rather macabre — playing with the 'Dance of Death'— he proceeded with his plan. He selected two prime plots in Gate of Heaven cemetery, with its majestic views. He chose Section 3, with two lots overlooking the lake.

As I'm wiping my father's stone, engraved with his military title of Staff Sergeant in front of his name, I feel compelled to catch him up on the latest family battles. I tell him that I stopped by the Greenview Café this morning, for old times' sake. *You won't believe this, Dad. It's gone now. They bulldozed the whole damn thing. Nothing there now but six inches of black asphalt. Just a fucking parking lot.* I enjoy using salty language with him, it's a kind of bond we share, knowing that we have both suffered through the agony of internalizing The Rules, and we mutually appreciate the work we have done to parse out all of the nuances and contradictions. We deserve these moments of shared idiolect. I sense that he gets the kind of special connection I'm invoking.

And of course he'll respond in like kind. I can hear a faint voice, giving his verdict from the afterlife: *verdammt Idioten.* Good to know I can still channel Dad's voice in our own version of German. Dad and I will always share this, *what do you call it in German? Verzweiflung? Hoffnungslosigkeit? Unmöglichkeit?*— the heartbreak caused by the inattentiveness of others, the grief of knowing that you will never be fully understood.

I give Dad's grave marker a final pat and then scooch on my knees over to my mother's stone, hoping she hadn't heard us swearing just now. I give her the extra spray of Windex that she deserves. *Pchit pchit pchit, pchit.* As I'm scrubbing between the letters of her name, I recall that we have some gardening news to catch up on. I tell her that I dropped by to see her old garden at her house. *Those little chicks and hens you planted on that little hill behind the porch — that's what you call them right? Chicks and hens?* — Hens and chicks, she corrects me. *Well, your hens and chicks, they're changing color now, so many shades of red and purple.* Scarlet and Burgundy, she says, tweaking my recollection. *Yes, yes, scarlet and burgundy, I didn't know colors like that even existed!*

I feel her nodding, the way that a teacher does when a student finally "gets" the point: *Of course, they do. But they surprise you every time you see them, like you're noticing them for the first time.* Yes, they do, I concur.

I feel myself standing up, as if pulled by a puppeteer, again observing myself from behind and above. When I lived in West Africa, I learned an important lesson about dying and communication with those who have passed on. In Éwé tradition, the recently departed whose time on earth overlaps with people still here are the *zamani*, the living dead. They are not actually dead, for they still live within us, within those who knew them, those who were touched by them. We can call them to mind at will, create their likenesses in art, and insert them as living characters into a story at any moment.

However, when the last living person to know an ancestor dies, that ancestor leaves the *zamani* and migrates to the *sasha*, the realm of the revered dead. At that point, when our ancestors join the *sasha*, we no longer speak to them directly. They are not to be forgotten, of course, but to live on as an esteemed part of our ancestry.

My housekeeping task accomplished, and the gravestones sparkling as if brand-new, I start to gather myself to leave and stand upright. Realizing that conversation etiquette is not really necessary, I blurt out: *I have a question before I go. What's the meaning of…of all this?* I open my arms outward in a kind of ballet gesture.

I figure they must know the answer.

It's your रासयात्रा, my father says.

My what? My father is speaking in tongues!

Your rasa yatra. It's your journey, my father says.

I'd say more like a dance, but okay, journey, my mother concedes.

Or evolution, my father adds.

Or story to tell, my mother chimes in, reminding me of my birthright.

I nod in affirmation, somehow understanding.

She continues, *Gratitude. You just have to use all of this as a gift. Be grateful that you experienced it, all of it, including the grief.*

My father concurs. *Acceptance. Embrace everything, including the… pain. It's a beautiful journey if you do.*

I'm about to ask "Why? Why didn't you say these things earlier?"

The answer seems to be swirling in the air. *Feel reverence for the unknown, the unknowable.*

My hands naturally fold into the *atmanjali mudra* prayer position. A gesture of tribute.

Though I am but a…sh-shu-shu…sh-shu-shu….

I feel the breeze shifting directions, now blowing across the grass toward me, across the polished black gravestones. The wind is whispering, *It's time for you to go.*

I reach down to pick up the roll of paper towels that I've left on the ground between their gravestones. I tuck the roll of towels under my left arm and pick up the half-full bottle of blue Windex with my right hand, letting it hang by the nozzle from my index finger, revolving it like a sharpshooter might twirl a pistol. Annie Oakley at Gate of Heaven Cemetery.

For a moment I feel a chill and I look behind me. I see a line of golden gates, perched quietly atop seven hills, aligned one behind the other. The wind is blowing through them, and they begin to fade, disappearing down to their bones, magically, gracefully.

I turn forward. I begin to stroll across the rolling hills of the cemetery, with its arches of swaying sycamores, now empty of their golden leaves. I feel a spring in my step and bounce lightly back to my rented car, a white Ford Taurus, parked neatly at the edge of the road.

As I pull the keys out of my pocket and step onto the pavement, I see a clump of once-purple spiderworts, their flowers now faded to brown. I smile. It is one last offering. As a child when I walked through our garden with my mother, she would always point out where to look, where to detect a gift that nature was providing.

How could dying flowers be a gift? I wondered. She had the perfect answer: When flowers wither and die, they *always* create new life. If we look closely, sometimes the very things that are broken and vanishing before our eyes are also at the same time about to burst with unexpected beauty, exquisite beyond words.